I0533724

The Community:

Existence

A Novel By Jessie Mahoney

ISBN: 978-0-578-07828-1

This is a work of fiction. All characters and events portrayed in this book are fictional, and any resemblance to real people or incidents is purely coincidental.

THE COMMUNITY: EXISTENCE

Copyright 2010 Jessie Mahoney

All rights reserved, including the right to reproduce this book or portions thereof in any form.

For my parents, because Mom always had a book in her hand.

For Mr. Stuart Wood who taught me that reading could be so much fun.

For Sensei, for giving me the tools to follow my dreams.

And for Ed, who never stops believing in me.

"Frozen inside without your touch, without your love

Darling.

Only you are the life among the dead."

-- Evanescence

Prologue

Mikey and Stevie met at the corner in downtown Pellman and waited for J.J. to finish up with the young girl buying her stash from him. After about a minute J.J. planted a deep kiss on her red-painted lips and sent her across the street to stand under the street light. He motioned for them to come closer. Mikey took a look at the girl across the street and smiled, "Damn J.J., that one is sweet!"

J.J. laughed and knocked knuckles with his two friends. "You have no idea, man. Time for her to start earning her keep though, y'know what I mean?"

"I hear dat, man." Mikey casually glanced around. "You got my shit?"

J.J. nodded, "How much you got to spend?"

"Forty, between the two of us."

"You havin' a party I don't know about?" J.J. asked.

"Nah, man, just meetin' some honeys later and wanna have a good time."

J.J. nodded, "Tell you what I'm gonna do Mikey, I need some new rides for the new business, older models, nuthin' too fancy. You get those for me and we'll work out some deals in the future."

Mikey looked at Stevie who nodded back. "Yeah, man, whatever you want."

As they made their exchange, a large, white sedan pulled up next to J.J.'s new girl across the street. They watched her get into the car before it drove away. "That didn't take long," the pimp said with a smile.

*****

Amanda fastened her seat belt and tried not to look at the old man who had picked her up. Instead she concentrated on how nice the car was, thankful that he didn't try to talk to her. When she got to wherever they were going, she would slip away to the bathroom and allow the drugs she had just gotten to take over. In the morning, tonight would barely be a memory.

The old man drove the car through a pair of iron gates and down a long driveway before stopping in front of a large home on the water. Amanda had never seen a house so immense. She had been so awed by it that she hadn't even noticed that the old man had gotten out of the car and was now opening the door for her. She couldn't help but smile at the gesture. At least he had class, maybe tonight wouldn't be so horrible after all.

"Come along, my dear," he said when he offered her his hand.

Amanda hesitated but took his hand and let him lead her into the house. "Um..." she started, "I should tell you... I'm sorta new at this..."

The old man laughed a little and patted her hand still in his. "Don't worry, my dear, tonight I only look for someone to share a warm cup of tea with." He walked Amanda into a parlor where there was a small round table set up with expensive looking tea cups. He held out a chair for her. "And perhaps some nice conversation."

Amanda smiled and sat down, wondering if it was real gold

that was trimming the rims of the cups and saucers in front of her. "Well, just so you know, Mister, it's still the same price– "

"Yes, yes, I know." He waved a dismissive hand in the air as he took his own seat. "And please, call me David." He poured them both some tea. "Do you take milk, or do you prefer honey?"

Amanda shifted uncomfortably in her chair. She really didn't know which she preferred since she couldn't recall ever having a cup of tea before. She shrugged her shoulders, somewhat embarrassed.

David smiled kindly. "Surely, someone as sweet as you must prefer honey."

"Thank you," Amanda said softly. All this kindness was starting to make her feel a little on edge. She wondered where the bathroom was as she thought of the drugs in her pocket.

David placed some biscuits on a dish and gave it to Amanda. She took it gratefully and vigorously ate two of them without looking up. Food didn't come easily these days, and any money she made went toward supporting her drug habit or J.J., rarely ever food. "How old are you my dear?" She heard him ask.

Amanda looked up, suddenly remembering where she was. She swallowed a mouthful of cookie before answering, "Fifteen."

David shook his head and sighed. "So young," he said almost inaudibly. He looked thoughtful then, and just for a moment there was something in his eyes that seemed to tell Amanda to run away before it was too late. But just as quickly, it was gone and David lifted his teacup, motioning Amanda to do the same. She did so and never noticed that David simply watched her from over his own cup, never drinking it himself.

Amanda thought that she had never before tasted anything so good as the tea and she quickly finished it along with two more biscuits. It warmed her from the inside and she felt more relaxed, not even worrying about how she was going to sneak away to do the drugs J.J. had given her.

David stood and held out his hand to her once again. "Come, my dear, there's something I would like to show you."

This time Amanda took his hand without hesitation, marveling to herself at how there really were kind people left in this world, people who didn't always want something from you.

She stood and was surprised when she wavered and fell against his chest. Instead of wondering why she was so lightheaded she found herself thinking about how strong this old man felt under his white suit jacket.

David didn't seem to notice her clumsiness, but quickly steadied her, guiding her into the kitchen. He walked slowly and deliberately, as if he expected her to not be able to keep up otherwise. "Did you know, my dear, that I can make a light bulb as bright as the sunlight?" He opened a door that led down a flight of stairs. "That's how I made all my money, by grabbing hold of power and making it even *more powerful.*

Amanda got dizzy just looking down the staircase that seemed to lead into an unending abyss. Her head was swimming now and she felt herself walking those steps, rather, practically being carried down them. She once again thought of how strong David was for someone his age. He was saying something about light bulbs and movies. Suddenly she reached the bottom and David flipped a switch. The hallway they were in lit up so brightly that Amanda needed to shield her eyes.

Amanda felt a startling urge to flee, run right back up those steps and never look back, but she didn't seem to be in control of her body anymore. She was streetwise enough to realize she had been drugged. Somewhere deep inside, her flight or fight mechanism was kicking in and there was nothing she could do about it. She felt panic rise in her throat as she watched David unlock a metal door.

"Tell me, my dear," he said as he faced inside the extremely brightly lit room, gently pushing Amanda ahead of him into it, "do you believe in monsters?"

Amanda heard the metal door slide shut behind her. Groggily she noticed a young man standing inside a square of darkness. "Hello?" she slurred.

The lights went out.

Outside the door David stood and listened until the screams died down to nothing.

Chapter 1

Forsythea Daniels had just made the biggest decision of her twenty-five years. She had up and left her only home in Lake George, NY for a chance at a new life as a freelance photographer on Long Island. With the trust money her grandfather had left for his only granddaughter, she had secured a place to live and a new lease on life.

She was in a town called Pellman, infamous for its dark deeds in the seedier parts of downtown, as well as its beautiful village with performing arts and lush shops on main street, and large estates on the water. Thea longed to enter into investigative reporting, but jobs in the field were scarce and competitive. She had befriended Joshua Myers, a reporter for the *Pellman Chronicle* who often arranged some work for her since the small paper was without a full time photographer. Since Pellman was a town where one could get anything one wanted, often at the off-the-truck discount store, Joshua had suggested that Thea get her hands on a police scanner so she could get to crime scenes quickly to get the juiciest pictures of the scene in progress. She was on her way to one now, a robbery on Main Street. It was an hour past dusk.

When she reached the address she saw a group of onlookers in front of the shop; the village police were shoving them off to one side. Thea wore her press badge and started snapping pictures of the police, the shop owners and the scene around her.

It was a small children's clothing store, not what you would think would attract the attention of a street thug. How much cash could there really be? Movement out of the corner of her eye turned her attention to the alleyway two buildings east of *Dragonfly's Children's Shop.* Hoping for an eyewitness, Thea started to walk toward it.

She could see cigarette smoke swirling about in the dim street light. Her heels clicked on the sidewalk and she slowed when she approached the opening to the alleyway. "Hello?" she called trying not to sound as nervous as she was. "Excuse me,

I'm with the press and I was wondering if you saw anything strange here tonight?" She could smell the cigarette now.

A man slowly stepped to the edge of the alley, but not quite out of it. He took a drag of his cigarette and blew out the smoke before he answered her. "Who are you?" He asked with an British accent.

Thea found herself wishing she had just stayed in front of the shop. Assuring herself that the police were only a few hundred yards behind her, she straightened and forced herself to continue, "My name is Thea and I work for the *Pellman Chronicle*," a small lie, "and you are?"

The man flicked his cigarette to the side and leaned against the wall. "Name's Edric."

Thea was thankful he had stayed where he was. She was having a difficult time keeping her nerves under control, what the hell was she doing in a dark alleyway with this man? She cleared her throat and shifted her weight nervously. "Well, Edric, may I ask you a few questions about what happened here tonight?"

The man named Edric sauntered silently across to Thea until he was toe to toe with her. "And what exactly do you think happened here tonight, Red?" he asked in a low tone.

Thea's hands reflexively tucked her auburn hair behind one ear. Her heart raced. His icy blue eyes mesmerized her and his sultry voice gave her chills. He at once excited and terrified her. He stood at least 6 feet tall with short dark hair. He was dressed in black jeans and a royal blue button down shirt, covered in a black leather jacket. Thea was frozen where she stood. "The uh, the robbery at the, um... children's shop." Her own stammering mortified her, but she just could not seem to gain control of her own voice.

Edric smiled. "Right, the robbery. Can't say that I saw anything of interest to your paper, Red."

Thea took a deep breath, taking in the aroma of tobacco and leather. "Well, okay then; I'll just be getting back to the scene." She took two steps back, not taking her eyes off of Edric, not trusting him and at the same time wanting to remember him.

"You do that, Red." When she turned away he called after her, "Hey Red!"

Thea turned around again to face him. She noticed he had gone back into the darkness of the alleyway. "What?"

"You be careful around here at night. Not everyone is as innocent as you are."

Before she could become completely enraptured in the power of this strange man's eyes, Thea turned and quickly headed back to the safety of the shop to take more pictures.

*****

Edric watched her go before turning back to his work. He strode behind the dumpster and picked up the young girl by her hair. She had been unconscious but quickly awoke when he grabbed her. She began flailing and spitting at him. "Let me go!"

"Not until you answer some questions." He slapped her, sending her flying into the brick wall behind her. She looked to be about 15 and was wearing the clothes she had stolen from the shop down the street; the tags were still on them.

She turned, holding her jaw and laughing. "What do you want?"

"I want his name."

"Screw you!" She yelled as she came off the wall and scratched at Edric's eyes, drawing blood.

Edric's eyes narrowed. "Here's how things work around here," he approached her like the predator he was, forcing her to step back toward the brick wall behind her. "*I* am the law." His slap came so quickly the girl hadn't a chance to defend herself. She staggered to her left. "*I* am the judge." *SMACK!* This time a backhand that caused the girl to whirl around to her right, catching herself on a dumpster. Edric pinned her up against the wall, his forearm on her throat. "And *I* am the executioner. Now, when I ask you a question, you *answer* me," he seethed at her. "Who made you?"

For a moment he thought this time he would get an answer, but then the little bitch apparently had delusions of grandeur, just like the rest of them had. She spit in his face and laughed at him again.

He threw her up against the opposite wall with enough force to send her flying with her feet off the ground.

The young girl fell to the ground and held her head. She slowly straightened as she stood and turned to face her attacker. Her eyes turned crimson and fangs protruded from her young lips as she hissed at him. She leapt for his throat.

Edric was tired of holding back. This kid wasn't going to give him any names. Before she had even bounced off the wall, he knew she had changed. "Want to play with the big boys, eh?" His own eyes turned scarlet and he easily dodged her lunge and shoved her forward throwing more power into her movement so that she rammed into the brick wall behind him. She spun wildly.

"What's the matter?" Edric sneered, "Daddy not teaching you how to fight off the bigger baddies than you?" He was on her in a flash and punched her in the face, feeling bone crush under his knuckles. She fell to the pavement. He continued his advancement on her. "Not teaching you how to stay outta sight!" He kicked her in the ribs.

The girl crawled away from him. This time when she turned to face him her human facade was out. She looked pathetic to Edric; how many humans could she lure in with those young eyes? "Please, Mister, I just want to go home," she pleaded in her most childlike voice.

Edric bent down to her and lifted her chin. "What's his name?" He asked again, this time with his own fangs bared.

She spit in his face and laughed before kicking him in the stomach.

Edric had had enough. He took out the wooden stake from his pocket and drove it into her heart through her back as she attempted to crawl away from him. She burst into a cloud of flames that quickly dwindled to nothing but ashes.

"Welcome to the Community; stupid child," he said to himself as he lit another cigarette. He heard the sound of cars starting and looked out of the alley to see the three police cars pulling away from the scene of the robbery. All this attention so the kid could get some new clothes. His eyes fell on the form of the slim redhead that had come to speak with him. She got into a car and drove off, watching him as she passed. The demon inside of him stirred at the memory of her scent, her milky white skin and the feelings of fear and excitement he had elicited from her. His heightened senses picked up the slightest change in her heartbeat, and it made his demon want more.

He had always remained careful not to bring too much attention to himself where the humans were concerned, contented to live quietly within the Community he had built. But this one was different, there was something about her that tugged at him. He would watch her, that much he was sure of.

Chapter 2

"Impressive, Miss Daniels," Mr. Wood, Editor in Chief of the *Pellman Chronicle* said as he wrote out a check. "You have a good eye." He ripped off the check from the pad. "And excellent timing." He smiled as he looked at her over his glasses.

"Thank you, Mr. Wood," Thea replied. She tried not to look as if she wanted to do a ridiculous happy dance at receiving her biggest check yet. She placed the check into the wallet in her purse. "Is there anything else you would like me to take a look at for you?"

"I could use a photographer for the beautification piece, Boss." Josh had just walked into the office.

"Beautification piece?" Thea asked.

Mr. Wood huffed. "Yeah, like they're gonna be able to make downtown Pellman into anything different from what it is, just by cleaning up a few buildings." He turned to his own computer. "Sure, Josh, Miss Daniels can partner up with you on it."

"Great." Josh smiled as he led Thea out of the editor's office.

"Oh my goodness, Josh thank you so much. I don't know what to say."

"Hey, you're a great photographer who can sketch as a bonus." Josh said as he walked back to his desk. He grabbed a stack of papers from a drawer, placed them into an envelope and handed it over to Thea. "Here's a basic outline of the story, who I want to interview, where I think some photos should be taken, take a look at them and we'll meet for lunch and go over our game plan tomorrow."

Thea's heart raced with excitement. "Thank you so much Josh, you've been a real big help to me since I've been down here. You won't be disappointed."

"I'm sure I won't," he smiled.

The October sun was already beginning to set as Thea made her way out to her car in the parking lot behind the office of the

Chronicle. She couldn't believe her luck. She had just finished selling a set of pictures from the robbery the night before and was already asked to help out on another project. She smiled broadly at her quick success in the market so far, reminding herself to take Josh out to dinner as soon as her check cleared.

As she neared her car, her body instinctively slowed and became tense. The hairs on the back of her neck stood on end, causing a cold chill to run through her. She took in the scenery around her. She couldn't see anything out of place, but thought that picking up the pace to her car wouldn't do any harm. She broke into a jog and swiftly got out her keys from her coat pocket.

Suddenly, arms were around her and she heard two male voices laughing. "Where you goin', pretty mama?" One said into her ear before throwing her into the arms of his partner. "Catch, Mikey!"

The second man caught her and spun her so that she was up against her own car, his body inches from hers. "Is this your car?" he sneered. He grabbed the keys from her hand. "These your keys?"

She nodded her head. "Yes, take it, go ahead." She winced at the man's odorous breath and closed her eyes. She heard him say to his partner, "Look at that, Stevie, we got ourselves a ride for the night." He laughed briefly but stopped when he heard no response. "Stevie?"

Thea opened her eyes and watched as the smelly man called Mikey turned around and came face to face with Edric, the man from the alleyway the night before. Where had he come from? Edric smiled evilly. "'Ello, mate. You seem to have something of mine."

Something about the dark haired man made Mikey go cold. His mouth went dry but he managed, "Where's Stevie?"

Edric grabbed the man by the lapels and spun him around, lifting him off the ground. He emitted a low growl and let his eyes change their hue. "She is not to be touched," he warned, "by any of you vermin. Or I *will* find you, Michael."

When his feet were firmly on the ground Mikey made a mad dash out of the lot and away from the monster he swore was on his heels. Edric easily pushed his demon down and turned to find Thea clutching at her jacket near her slender neck. He stepped closer but stopped when he noticed the grip on her jacket tighten."You all right, Red?"

She nodded but did not look up at him. She wanted to cry but didn't want him to see her do it. She turned and tried the handle to her car to no avail, still locked. She buried her head in her hands and began to quietly weep.

Edric sighed and scooped up the keys dropped by the mugger. He softly came up behind her and, reaching around her tense body, gently placed the keys in her hand.

Thea took a deep breath and seemed to settle when Edric got close to her and gave her the keys. She composed herself and turned to thank him but he had already disappeared into the night. Not for the first time, she found herself wondering about this man. She quickly got into her car and promptly locked her doors. She took three more deep breaths before driving off.

Edric watched her leave from the shadows. He wanted nothing more than to follow her home and have her all to himself. But he knew that was his demon and he did all he could to suppress it, most of the time. He turned his attention back to the derelict that had attacked his redhead. Every once in awhile he needed to allow his demon a little recreation, lest it consume him. Tonight would be one of those nights, but first he needed to know something. He glared at the petrified man huddled against the dumpster and could smell the odor of freshly spilled urine. "Who's been taking the children?" Edric asked calmly.

Stevie shook his head, trying to wake up from this nightmare he had found himself in. All he had wanted to do tonight was score some hits, now he felt like he was on the worst trip of his life.

Edric rolled his eyes at the pathetic man. Didn't humans have any spine these days? He pulled the man up by his hair to gain his attention. "Look at me," he commanded.

Stevie looked up and started to cry, fearing his end. "Please man....," he begged.

"Sshhh," Edric soothed, "Tell me who has been taking the kids. Is there someone new in town? Tell me what you know and you might just live through this night."

"Nobody new in town, man, I swear, I don't know nuthin'!"

Edric bared his fangs and hissed for effect.

"Oh my God! Oh Jesus! Wait, wait! Please! I might know somethin'!" Stevie backed himself closer to the dumpster.

Edric allowed his human mask to come forth and smiled. "There now, was that so hard? Who is it?"

Stevie seemed to calm slightly at the kinder face. "I don't know the guy's name or nuthin', but every Saturday there's this rich looking dude that sits on the bench at the park and he just sits there and watches the kids hangin' out, y'know? Like some sorta sicko, y'know? Maybe that's the guy, right?"

Edric thought for a moment. "During the day?"

Stevie nodded furiously. "Now can I go man? I did what you asked, y'know, told you what you needed to know, so can I go man? Please man? I won't tell nobody about you, y'know?" He had started to cry again.

Edric placed a hand on the man's shoulder assuredly. "You did good, Stevie, you did good." He stepped closer though and Edric felt his demon twitch, it needed to feed. "But there's still this thing about you handling my redhead out there."

Stevie's eyes widened and his scream was cut short as the full face of Edric's demon leaned in to devour him.

*****

The next day was Saturday and the first thing Thea did that morning was go shopping. Living in a town such as Pellman where the crime rate was pretty high, it wasn't difficult to find a gun shop close by. She quietly entered *Long Island Guns and Ammo* and walked up to the middle aged man at the desk.

"Can I help you, young lady?" He asked politely in his southern drawl that seemed more than a little out of place in New York. Thea wondered where he was from.

She gestured toward the front of the store. "The sign in the window says you sell tasers and stun guns?"

The gentleman smiled. "We sure do. Which were you interested in?"

Thea was confused. "Which what?"

"Well, are you looking for a taser or a stun gun?"

"Aren't they the same thing?"

"No ma'am. A stun gun needs direct contact maintained and the pain is localized to the point of contact." He walked over to a shelf, took down a box and brought it over to the counter where Thea joined him. "This here's what you're looking for. Much more powerful than a traditional stun gun and has a firing zone of up to fifteen feet. There's a laser sight so you know where you'll be hitting your target. This device will incapacitate the assailant for thirty seconds. And if you needed to, just drop the taser and get to safety."

"Just leave it there?"

"Yes Ma'am. This particular model comes with a replacement guarantee. If you lose it during an attack, the manufacturer will replace it for free; as long as you filed a police report, that is."

Thea held the taser in her hand. "It's so light," she marveled.

"It sure is. Just another great feature. It's about six inches long and only weighs about seven ounces. Easy enough to be carried around in your purse or even coat pocket."

Thea thought about actually using the taser on the men that had tried to mug her the night before. "I don't know, what about something like pepper spray?"

The man sighed and shook his head. "Let me ask you, Ma'am, what if the wind is blowing in your direction? How effective do you think that spray will be then? I am telling you, a pretty lady like yourself living in a town like this, ought to have herself a reliable self defense tool, and that's what this is."

Thea nodded her head. "Well, you've got me sold."

The man beamed and went to the shelf again. "I think I have just the right one for you." He came back with a different box. "They even come in pink."

Thea couldn't help but smile. Four hundred dollars later she was now armed (sort of) and slightly dangerous. Well, at least more prepared than she was last night.

She lived in a small one bedroom apartment just outside the village. It wasn't as nice as Main Street and the more expensive areas of Pellman, but it certainly was not south of Main where all the drug addicts and prostitutes hung out. When she got home from shopping she took out the taser gun and tried to get used to how it felt in her hand. The man at the shop had suggested she play with it, with the power disabled of course, to get the feel of it. So she practiced taking it in and out of her purse, and then in and out of her jacket pocket.

Just as she decided that she wasn't sure that the weapon would ever feel comfortable, she heard a knock on her door. Her heart jumped into her throat and she clutched at the taser as she approached the eye hole.

She saw Josh standing on the other side of the door. "Uh... just a minute," she called, taking in a sweeping glance of the apartment, searching for anything out of place before she let him in. She opened the door. "Hi Josh, I totally forgot we were meeting to go over the project today." She opened the door wider. "Come on in, I'll just be a minute getting ready."

Josh entered the small dwelling and proceeded to look around while Thea busied herself in the bathroom. He was happy to see that Thea was a neat person, he hated working with unorganized people. He sat himself down on the couch and waited.

Thea brushed her hair and teeth and straightened her clothes, glad she had decided to wear her new jeans today. At least she looked neat. She hadn't known Josh long but so far he had been very helpful in getting her career off to a good start. She wanted to look professional enough so that he would recommend the paper use her for future projects as well.

Josh stood when she came out of the bathroom. He smiled and opened the door. "Shall we?"

Thea grabbed her leather satchel and together they made their way down to the front doors of the lobby.

"I'll drive," Josh offered. He gestured to his red Chrysler Sebring convertible.

Thea got in and buckled her seat belt. "You're not going to believe what happened to me last night." Thea related her horrific story of the night before, as Josh drove them to the coffee house in the village. The day was warm but completely overcast.

"Have you called the police yet?" Josh asked when they got their drinks and sat at a table near the window.

Thea shook her head. "I haven't; but I don't think I could describe them to anyone; I didn't get a very good look at either of them." She took a sip of her coffee and smiled a little. "And then out of nowhere this man shows up and chases them away."

"What man?"

"This guy that I talked to the night of the robbery. His name is Edric."

"I still think you should call the police and report it," Josh said. "If nothing else maybe they'll patrol the parking lot a little so it doesn't happen again."

"I'm just glad it's over." She took a clearing breath. "But enough of this, let's talk about the story we're doing."

Josh took out his notebook and went over the premise of the Beautification Project. "They basically are trying to clean up Downtown Pellman in the hopes of getting rid of the riffraff and bringing in some nicer shops so people bring some money into that part of town." He sat back in his chair and looked at Thea thoughtfully. "Listen, we are going to be interviewing some very upscale people in the community, most of whom are men," he said. "I think you should consider wearing skirts when we do, it makes a woman look more professional," he said.

"What?" She shook her head slowly and said, "oh no, I don't really feel comfortable in skirts or dresses."

"Why not?"

She felt heat rise to her cheeks. "I don't know, I just never did I guess."

"Thea, you would look great in a skirt, and these guys are old fashioned pillars of the community type. I just think we would get more out of the interview if they had a woman there who looked the part of a professional from their perspective," Josh said. "It's just a suggestion."

She smiled in spite of herself. "Well, thank you Josh, I'll take it into consideration."

Thea's sudden discomfort caused her to look away from Josh and out the window, needing to squint to make sure she was seeing correctly. Across the street was the Village Square Park where families often brought their children to play on the playground. She could swear she saw a familiar figure dressed in a leather jacket, standing under a large maple tree, smoking a cigarette. She snapped her attention back to Josh. "Oh my Gosh! There he is! The guy that scared off those two men last night."

Josh leaned forward. "What? Where?"

"Right over there under that tree. I'm going to go talk to him." Thea stood and put on her jacket. "Don't worry, I'll take the bus home. I'll call you later." And with that she rushed out of the shop, and dashed across the street.

Edric hated being out in the daytime, but at least it was overcast and there was enough foliage left on the tree he waited under to add a little shade when necessary. He had just fed, so even on a cloudless day he could stay out for a little while without causing any harm to himself. He heard her coming before she was more than 200 feet from him. He couldn't help a smile cross his lips. His demon stirred. "'Ello, Red."

Thea walked up to Edric and smiled. "I didn't know if I would ever see you again," she said. "I wanted to thank you for yesterday. I don't know what would have happened if you hadn't come along."

Edric took a final drag from his cigarette before throwing it in the dirt, crushing it into the ground with the heel of his black boots. "You're welcome." He went back to watching the park.

"I actually went out and bought a taser this morning, but I don't know if I'll ever be able to use it." She shuffled her feet in the dirt and wondered if Edric thought she should wear skirts too.

In the daylight she could get a better look at him even though he wore dark sunglasses. He was very fair skinned with short black hair that was thick and threatened to curl if any longer. She found it difficult to guess his age. He looked young, in his early 30s perhaps, but there was an air about him that made him seem worlds older than that. "You know, we keep meeting up and I don't even know if you know my name."

"Your name is Thea and you work for the *Pellman Chronicle*." He said without taking his attention away from the park.

"Oh," she said, a little surprised he had remembered their first meeting so well. "And you're Edric, right?"

Edric looked at her now and grinned. He took a small step closer to her. "Yes, Red, but you already knew that, didn't you?" He went back to watching the park. After a few seconds he asked in a more serious tone, "did they hurt you?"

Thea felt her body tense at the memory of yesterday's events. Now it was her turn to watch the park. "A little, but mostly just scared me, that's all."

His jaw tightened, wishing he had kept the man alive for a day so he could kill him tonight. "I'm sorry I didn't get to you sooner."

Thea looked at him in disbelief. "Are you kidding? Edric you saved my life last night, and I could never repay you for what you did. I don't think they would have just let me go." Her voice trailed off at the end, not wanting to think about what might have been. She finally noticed that he had been staring into the park. "Are you looking for someone?"

"Yes."

Not much for conversations, this one. "A friend?"

"No." Edric had been leaning against the tree but now he straightened as he watched an old man enter the park and sit on the bench near the playground. He paid particular attention to a group of young teens milling about by the far fence, probably smoking weed. Yes, that would be who he would want. Strung out teenagers who are about to or have already left home, their families half expecting them to come up missing, thinking it only a matter of time, if they had families of their own at all. That's how he stays under the radar. Too many young junkies in this town. But he was human, Edric could tell even from where he stood.

Thea followed his gaze. "Is that the man you're looking for?"

Edric looked at her and took of his sunglasses. His piercing blue eyes locked on hers. "Now you listen to me, Red, don't you ever go talking to that man over there, you hear me?"

She couldn't even blink when she looked into those eyes. She nodded her head, her breath catching a little at his sudden intensity. "Who is he?" she managed.

Edric stepped closer to her, taking in her beauty in the day. She was incredibly sexy in her form fitting jeans, and her white blouse made him want to hold her close to him. He swept her with his eyes. There was a man's scent on her. He met her eyes again. "Were you on a date?" he asked.

"What? Um... no," she stammered. "Just having coffee with a colleague."

His eyes narrowed. "And where is Romeo now?" He did not like the thought of her with another man, colleague or not.

Thea glanced back at the coffee shop; someone else occupied the table she and Josh had been sitting at. "I, um..." She turned back to Edric. "I excused myself and came over to thank you for saving my life last night."

Edric visibly softened and lifted the right corner of his mouth in a half smile, a gesture that sent a pleasant chill through Thea's stomach. He put his sunglasses back on and began to slowly walk out of the park. He stopped and turned to her. "You coming?"

Thea fell into step alongside until they stopped at a 1970s style black Oldsmobile Cutlass Supreme with mirrored windows. "Is this your car?"

"Yes." He walked around to the driver's side.

"It's big." Thea noticed there was barely a spec of dust on it.

"I like big back seats." He opened the door and stood facing her.

"Oh." Thea said simply, then she thought about his statement and blushed. "Oh!"

He smiled at her reaction. "Get in, Red."

"Oh I probably shouldn't." *You're damn right you shouldn't! You don't even know this guy!* A little voice inside her head yelled at her.

"I'll drive you home," he said, "that's all."

Thea smiled in spite of her angry conscience. "Promise?"

Edric said nothing but shot her a smile that made her stomach flip pleasurably, as he stepped into the car. Thea decided to get in, not wanting to stand around and wait for the next bus. There was something about Edric that made her feel safe.

She put on her seat belt. "Thank you." The engine roared to life and he pulled away from the curb, following the directions Thea gave him to her apartment complex; they would be there in minutes. "So," she started. "Where are you from?"

"Around."

"Around where?"

Edric gave her a sideways glance before answering, "Originally from England, but I've been many places. Why do you want to know?"

"Just curious." She was quiet then, not knowing what else to say.

She didn't push the envelope. For a reporter she was too easily dissuaded from her task. "My turn," he said.

Thea looked at him in response.

"Is Thea your full name, or a nickname of sort?"

"It's actually short for Forsythea. It's silly, I know, it's just a plant."

"Not just a plant," he offered. "Prized for being beautiful, tough and reliable." He looked at her and she blushed again.

They pulled into her complex parking lot and Thea wondered if she should invite him up, but that would imply something more than she thought she was prepared to do. "Well, thank you, for everything." She opened her door.

"Be seeing you around, Forsythea."

And with that he was gone. Thea ran her fingers through her hair and walked up to her apartment on the second floor. She made her second sure fire decision since she had begun her new life: she would find out who this Edric was, and she would start by finding out who the man was in the park that Edric had been so interested in. She quickly grabbed her camera and ran back down the stairs and got into her car. She felt a rush of excitement running through her at the thought of investigating who this gentleman was.

She parked in the midst of other cars across from the park and was relieved to see that the older man was still there. He appeared to be on the phone. She attached her professional zoom lens to her camera, and proceeded to take pictures. With the telephoto lens she could make out more specifically what the man was doing. He wasn't on a call at all, but seemed to be trying to discreetly take pictures of some of the teenagers by the fence line. Thea focused in on them and she felt a wave of sadness wash over her. The kids were obviously smoking pot and dealing other drugs. The oldest couldn't have been more than sixteen and she thought one girl was as young as twelve. How could they get so lost so soon in their lives?

Thea put her camera down and wondered if this man was a child abductor or neighborhood watch. She started her car and drove back to her apartment where she could print out the pictures she had taken.

She found herself once again wondering about Edric. Was he a sort of community savior who is concerned about this man being some kind of pedophile? Or was he the top drug dealer, just trying to protect his underage dealers? To look at him he fit the description of the latter, but his actions thus far made her think he was the first. Did he think himself a vigilante? Thea was resolved to find out.

Chapter 3

Thea woke from another less than full night's sleep. She had gotten all the information she could about one Mr. David Francis Arthur, a fifty-seven year old man who had lost his only son six months ago in a boating accident; well, his boat had never been found and his son was presumed dead, or lost at sea. David's wife had succumbed to breast cancer the year before. He had no other surviving relatives. He was from a long line of well to do families and he spent much of his time researching more effective power sources and selling his ideas to larger companies. There wasn't much else about him. No kind of record with the police and not even that many outstanding good deeds. He seemed like just a regular guy who was possibly a little lonely, going to the park to people watch.

She wondered why Edric had been so adamant that she stay away from him. He obviously thought Mr. Arthur was dangerous, or at least a danger to Thea. Her next dilemma was how she was going to get this information to Edric? She had only ever seen him accidentally. She had no idea of where or how to find him. She didn't even know his last name.

It was Tuesday morning and she was to report to the *Chronicle* office to meet Josh before starting on their list of interviews for the day. She had decided to take his advice and wear a skirt. She chose a black A-line skirt with a red silk blouse and a matching black jacket. She wore nude stockings and a pair of black pumps. She looked great! She was also incredibly uncomfortable. She found it difficult to move easily, not because of the shoes, she could wear heels, but because she was so self-conscious about her figure. She was thin but not terribly curvy and always thought of herself as rather plain looking in the area of her body. Her green eyes were her best feature, she thought, in contrast with her dark auburn hair. She sighed heavily at herself in the mirror but was determined to go through with the outfit at least for the day.

They spent the afternoon developing a story on the Beautification Project of downtown Pellman. They interviewed the local town official as well as some of the shop owners along Main Street. After gathering some opinions from the local residents, the two decided to treat themselves to dinner at a local seafood restaurant on the water.

On their way back to the office parking lot so Thea could get her own car, they drove through the poorer parts of town. Josh told Thea that it was one of the areas on the town's list to "beautify." They slowed down a little as they passed a strip mall. "I think that's one of the stores on the project list," Josh pointed out.

Thea looked into the set of stores and her eyes widened at the sight of a familiar black Oldsmobile. She was suddenly very anxious to get to her own car. She simply nodded at Josh, hoping that he would read her signals and get back to the office.

Once in her own car, Thea drove herself back to the strip mall. She parked right next to Edric's car and looked at the stores that were there. There was a small grocery, a dollar store, two empty stores and then a seedy looking tavern called *Nightly's Pub*. Although she wished he was in the grocery, Thea was certain Edric would be at the bar. She grabbed the envelope on the front seat with the pictures and information she had gathered on David Arthur and followed her instincts.

She regretted her decision the moment she had gotten about ten feet from the pub. Two men in leather jackets stared at her as she slowly walked up to the door. She froze when the man with the shaved, tattooed head smiled and took a step toward her. "Now what's a pretty lady like you doing downtown?"

Thea's heart pounded and she couldn't think of anything to say, nor could she make her legs work. The other man grabbed his friend's arm and faced him. "No, Robert, can't you sense him?" Thea heard him say. "You know who she's here for."

Thea gathered some strength. "Do you know if Edric is here?" Her voice cracked. The man named Robert became suddenly very serious and walked back to the door, opening it for her. She took a deep breath to try to steady her heart and stepped through. The other man followed her in. She stopped in the doorway, wishing she hadn't come here at all. The room was filled with people Thea had never in her life associated with. All leather jackets, chains and tattoos, and all of them staring at her. She was so frightened she could barely breathe. She searched the room frantically and was relieved when she spotted Edric leaning up against the wall by the pool table. He saw her immediately and sauntered over, handing his pool cue to another man.

He glared at her when he faced her and Thea once again found herself caught by those icy blues. "Found her outside, Edric." The man said from behind her.

"Thank you, Liam." Then, to her he said, "outside. Now." She did as he commanded. Once out the door he grabbed her above the elbow and led her to her car. "Just what the bloody hell do you think you're doing here?"

"I'm... I'm sorry," she stammered, at once thankful to be out of the pub but at the same time feeling like a child being scolded. "I was driving by and I saw your car..."

"You were driving by this dive? I find that a little hard to swallow, Red." He lit a cigarette and then continued. "You are never to come here by yourself again, is that understood? You're a damn sight lucky that Liam was the one who was outside when you did."

She decided now was not the time to ask just how Liam had known she was there for Edric, but instead handed him the manila envelope.

He took it. "What's this now?" He opened up the seal and looked at the contents. He looked back up at Thea. "Where did you get all this?"

"I work for the paper, remember? I just thought getting some information about that man would help you. Just trying to repay a debt." Her voice trailed off and she took to studying her shoes.

Edric calmed down. He couldn't believe all that she was able to gather in only a matter of days. He was fairly certain she didn't have to hunt anyone down and threaten their lives for it either. "You didn't speak to him, did you?"

Thea shook her head. "No, I stayed away from him like you said. Although I don't think he's all that bad, just a lonely old man who lost his son recently."

Edric opened his own car and put the envelope inside to

inspect later. He turned back to face Thea and that's when he really noticed her. He stepped closer to her, hearing her heart rate quicken; it tempted his demon within. "Nice outfit, Red."

Thea shifted uncomfortably. "Do you," she cleared her throat nervously. "Do you like it?"

"Now why would you care if I liked it or not?" Another step closer, now capturing her green eyes with his.

"I don't know. It's a new look for me, just curious as to what you think." She spoke in a nervous whisper.

"I think," another step closer and now only inches between their bodies, "you look a bit uncomfortable in it."

Thea let out her breath. Had she been holding it? "I am, a little."

"Then why the change?"

"A friend suggested it. I don't know, I guess I was just worried about what people thought." She tore her eyes away from his finally, and looked down at her feet again.

Edric lifted her chin and looked at her with one eyebrow

raised. "If you must know, I like whatever you wear. You could try wearing less and ask my opinion on that too."

Thea let out a quick laugh and calmed down a bit. He had that effect on her, she noticed. She glanced back up at the pub they had come out of. "I'm sorry if I embarrassed you in front of your friends."

Edric never looked away from her. "You didn't embarrass me, Red, it's just a dangerous place for a girl like you."

She nodded. He was right of course, she had known that as soon as she saw Robert and Liam by the door. She sighed, "Well, sorry if I got you angry."

"No need to apologize, Luv, next time you want to go out for a few drinks, we'll pick a place more your speed." He smiled when she blushed.

Thea smiled back, pleasantly nervous at his suggestion. "I should go." She walked to the other side of her car.

Edric leaned up against his car and finished his cigarette. "If you say so."

Thea took in how sexy he looked right then and wondered what it would be like to kiss him. Before she got into her car she said, "Let me know if you need anything else."

He watched her drive away. She had courage coming here to find him, he had to appreciate that. Once inside his car, he took the contents of the envelope out again for a better look. The close-ups of the man interested him as did the pictures of the children he had been watching.

Edric had started noticing the occasional teen roaming around making a spectacle of themself about five months ago. He had tried to bring them into the Community, let them know the rules, but it was the sire's job to do that. He had never so much as gotten a name of the sire out of any of them and in the end he had killed them all. There had been eight so far. Thea had said the man had lost his son recently. So this David Arthur was bringing home some snacks for his late son, Edric was sure of it. He searched the papers Thea had given him and noticed that she had conveniently left out the man's address. No matter, he would find him nonetheless.

*****

It had been a week since the last time Thea had seen Edric, but not a day had gone by that she hadn't thought about him at one time or another. She wondered who he was, what was his story? She wanted to find out more about him but with just a first name to go on, so far she had come up empty.

It was five o'clock Tuesday evening when she had left the office after handing in the final pictures for the story. She hadn't eaten anything all day and decided to walk down two blocks on Main Street to a small brewery for a burger and fries. The sun was setting earlier and earlier as autumn pressed on, and darkness was already beginning to settle. She could hear the buzz of the street lamps coming to life as she walked.

When she passed by an empty shop her attention was caught by the sound of someone softly crying. She turned the corner into the walkway between buildings and saw a small girl squatting on the ground with her head in her hands. Her body shook with her sobs. Thea walked up to her and placed her hand on her shoulder. "Is everything all right?" she asked gingerly.

The little girl looked up at Thea with tear filled eyes, "I can't find my mom," she whimpered.

Thea thought that the girl must be about twelve years old and seemed familiar to Thea somehow. She put on her sweetest smile and stood, holding out her hand for the girl to take. "You can't? Well, I can help you find her. Come on, it's okay, I won't bite."

The girl smiled and stopped crying immediately. She held tightly to Thea's hand and with the other she pointed down the brick walkway toward the parking lot behind the shops. "I think she went down there." She gave a tug on Thea's hand and led her on.

Thea smiled down at the girl and went willingly with her. They both stopped short when a dark figure stepped out of the shadows and blocked their way. "Get away from her," the voice commanded.

Thea thought she recognized it. "Edric?" she asked.

Edric stepped closer. "I said, get your bleedin' hands off her!" he seethed.

At first Thea thought he was speaking to her, but then realized he was looking at the child when he spoke. Instinctively, Thea followed his leer and looked at the girl. Her breath caught at the sight before her. The soft brown eyes had turned red and, *my God are those fangs?* She tried to pull away but the girl's grip was like a vice on her hand. The thing that Thea had felt so sorry for a minute ago hissed at Edric and brought Thea's hand to her mouth in a flash, biting into her flesh. Thea screamed out in pain and terror.

Edric was suddenly right in front of them and he smacked the girl away from Thea, who staggered backward into the wall and slid down, watching on in disbelief. Quickly, Edric staked the child vampire and it exploded into flames, dissipating into dust. He looked over at the redhead. He could hear her heart racing and she was holding her hand against her chest chanting, "Oh my god, ohmygod, ohmygod..."

Softly Edric approached her. He bent down and turned her chin so that she looked at him. "You okay, Red?"

Thea stopped her rambling and focused on Edric. "What was

that?" she whispered.

"I don't have to tell you what that was, Luv, I already know you know a vampire when you see one." He helped her to her feet.

"I don't understand." Tears began to form in her eyes, but she tried not to panic. "That can't be. Can it?" Then realization dawned on her and her heart rate sped so much that she thought it might burst out of her chest. "Dear God she bit me! Oh my God, Edric she bit me!"

Edric gently took her wounded hand in his, blood was dripping freely from the bite marks in the fleshy part between her thumb and forefinger. "Sshhh," he soothed, "you can't be turned simply from a bite." He breathed in her scent and it intoxicated him. He took a step toward her, closing the distance between their bodies. "It's all right, Thea." He raised her hand to his lips as he spoke, locking her eyes with his. "We're not *all* about killing people." He licked the blood dripping from her hand and stopped at the bite marks left by the small vampire and gave a little suckle. He heard her breath catch and it was all he could do to keep his demon in check. By sheer force of will he stopped and pulled a handkerchief from his pocket. He tied it on her hand to stop the bleeding.

Thea thought that she had lost her mind. She had to be in a dream of some kind. She had been bitten by a little girl who was a... a vampire? And her savior, this Edric, who had come to her rescue, not for the first time, and did he just drink her blood?

When he sucked on her wound she felt her stomach flip erotically, and for a second she couldn't breathe. The next thing she knew he was tying a bandage to her hand. Their eye contact did not break for a second. "Edric...," she breathed, but couldn't bring herself to ask the question out loud.

Edric took another step closer, backing Thea up against the wall. "Yes ....?"

Another step and now Thea felt Edric press his body up against hers, eyes still locked, heart pounding. She needed to ask, had to know. "Are you...?"

Intoxicated by the fresh taste of her sweet blood, Edric allowed his demon its due, he would have more of her, even if it was just another taste. He pressed up against her, sensing her tension, her fear and above all else, her arousal. He softly brushed her hair away from her face and whispered, "yes." He cupped her face with his hand and captured her lips in a sensual kiss.

Thea felt electricity surge through her body at his touch. Passion held her lips that night for the first time in her life. His cool tongue searched for hers and found its willing partner. She felt his free hand finding its way up her pant leg to her hips, pulling them into him, then past her hips and up the outside of her blouse. He found her erect nipple through its satin prison and he rubbed his thumb over it, causing a whimper to escape her.

She couldn't deny the sensations her body was experiencing, but logic threatened, as always, *did he just admit to being a vampire? Whoa! Slow down there, Thea!* But she felt so good; never in her life had she felt such intensity. *Thea, we need to stop! Stop!* "Stop, stop!" She had torn away from his kiss and heard the words coming out of her before she even realized they were hers. "Please, Edric," she was out of breath and unable to look him in the eye for fear of being brought back into the heat she saw there.

Edric stopped his movements but did not move his position. He still pressed up against her and one hand held her just below her breast and the other still cupped her face, though he allowed her to look downward. It took all his internal might to push down his demon that wanted simply to possess her, right then, right there. He took an unnecessary breath, taking in her scent, memorizing it. Had he pushed too far? She liked it, there was no denying it, but she was so tense, not allowing herself to give in to her desires. He could hear her heartbeat becoming more steady. He kissed her on the forehead and left.

Thea just wanted to get her head together, to get control over her body. She felt drunk, dizzy with a whirlwind of emotions and desires. She dared not look at him. Was he disappointed? *So what! Vampire!* Was he turned off by her stopping him? *Can we go back to the fact that we think he's a vampire?* Yes, and there was that. But now she had doubts that any of that was actually real. Before she could muster the strength to look at him again she felt him kiss her forehead and then a breeze. When she looked up, he was gone. The only piece of him left was the handkerchief around her hand, a blood stain barely coming through the cloth. She brought it up to her lips and inhaled, smelling leather and tobacco. It was real, it had all been real. She spotted the pile of dust on the ground and shivered.

Thea didn't go into the office the rest of the week. She had told Josh that she wasn't feeling well, *no lie there,* and she had research for another paper to do. *Research, yes. Paper, no.* The bite marks on her hand were not taking as long as she would have thought to clear up. At this point they looked enough like taser burn marks and she had decided that would be her cover story if necessary. She had kept the handkerchief Edric had given her in her pocket, somehow feeling safer with a piece of him always within reach.

Her head was spinning at what she had gone through in the past two months, but mostly with the revelation that there were indeed things that went bump in the night. Not only that, but she seemed to have fallen into somewhat of a relationship with one. No wonder she couldn't find out anything about him in the database. She hadn't bothered going back more than forty years.

She was spending countless hours in the library researching anything she could find on the subject of vampires. She took to carrying a wooden stake in her pocket along with her taser, not sure if a taser would work on someone who was not even technically alive.

The day after the incident she had been absolutely bothered by something about the ... attack ... she had experienced the night before. The girl had looked somewhat familiar. It had been around noon when she had finally figured it out and had anxiously torn through the photos she had taken at the park. Sure enough the little girl along the fence line who had been doing drugs was the ... girl ... that had bitten her.

Then off to the local library she had gone to gather more information about... well, about vampires. Thea glanced at her watch and let out a sigh, five-thirty. Sunset was in half an hour; she had better get a move on if she wanted to be home by then. She had decided that she was never going out after dark ever again. The library was a block away from the park on Main Street and she'd had to leave her car all the way down there in the absence of closer spots. She put the books she had been looking through back, except for one, *Vampires and Folklore*. She signed it out, tucked it into her leather satchel and headed out of the library deep in thought.

Her thoughts lately made her head spin. She couldn't get a complete handle on the things she was experiencing. There was a part of her that fought every ounce of evidence that there were vampires, and that Edric was one of them. But then there was a part of her that simply accepted it for what it was. This same part wondered about Edric, would she ever see him again? Their moment together between the buildings on Main Street lingered with her always. She could feel his lips on hers, his hands making themselves at home with her body. Her stomach did a pleasant little flip again at the memory.

She was halfway to her car when she realized it was much darker than it should have been. She looked at her watch again, but it still read five-thirty. Thea brought the watch up to her ear and listened: silence. "Shit!" she cried, looking around nervously.

It was way passed five-thirty and sundown. Just my luck, she thought, way to go Thea. Okay, it's after dark in Pellman, apparently vampire capital of the world, and I'm out walking alone in the dark. "Shit!" she softy said again. She was halfway between the safety of the library and her car. Which way?

Taking a deep breath she forced herself to calm down and she quickened her pace as she continued to her car. She let out a small scream when she heard a twig snap from behind her. She whirled around and let out her breath when she found that there was no one (or no thing) there. Must have been the wind, she let herself think. Thea once again inhaled deeply and turned around to continue on her way and bumped right into a young man. Thea's breath caught in her throat as she gasped, expecting the worst.

"Hey Lady," the kid said as he grabbed her by the shoulders. "Watch where you're going, will ya?"

A little bit of relief spread over Thea at the teenager's complaint. Surely a vampire wouldn't complain like a normal kid. But the little girl had looked and acted normal the other night, and Edric seemed normal at first too. Thea panicked and dealt a swift knee to his groin and the kid fell to the ground on his knees. "Owww! What'd you do that for?"

Thea began to doubt herself. Maybe he wasn't a vampire; he wasn't threatening her at all. Did she just attack some innocent kid out for a walk? "Uh oh," she said softly. "Hey, I'm sorry. I thought you were... well, never mind. I'm really sorry." Thea touched his shoulder.

In an instant he grabbed her wrist and looked up at her; scarlet eyes and fangs that seemed too long for any animal. "Don't worry, pay back's a bitch."

"No!" Thea reacted quickly and pulled out her taser, stunning him right on the neck, loosening the grip he had on her enough so she could escape. She took advantage and sprinted off through the park before she even realized where she was going. She didn't need to look back to know he was right behind her. As she ran she screamed for help, hoping that Edric was out there, knowing he was the only one who could save her now. No help came.

Thea's lungs were burning with the need to breathe and although she tried to force herself to stay at top speed, she began to slow down. She ducked behind a large tree and prayed that the vampire hadn't seen her do so, hoping that she still had her thirty second window from the taser even on someone who was already technically dead.

She heard dry, fallen leaves crackling under footsteps from somewhere behind her. "I can hear you breathing," he teased.

Thea covered her mouth with her hands. She couldn't tell how close he was.

"I can feel your heart pounding," he continued.

Thea willed herself to be as still as she could. He seemed to be in a completely different area now. She felt panic settling in.

"I can smell your fear." Within seconds he was upon her, dragging her out from behind the huge elm by her hair, his face was inches from hers. "And it smells delicious."

Thea began to cry and attempted to fight him off by hitting and kicking as much as she could. The vampire laughed and then backhanded her across the face.

"No!" she screamed as she fell to the ground. "Somebody help me please!" She scrambled to get to her feet but he lifted her up by the shirt, ripping the material.

"That's it, bitch, scream louder. It makes this so much more fun."

"No, please don't do this. Somebody please help me!" Thea sobbed as the monster planted another blow to her face, knocking her down once more. Her cheekbone was on fire and she felt close to unconsciousness. Oh God, help me...

*****

Edric sat inside his home on the other side of the fence of the village park and listened to the struggle taking place there. Sounds like someone was going to feast tonight, he thought, knowing there was a vampire out hunting. He heard an angry vamp call someone a bitch, then a smack. He let out an aggravated sigh; no one hunted with dignity anymore. None of the fledglings were ever taught finesse these days.

"Somebody help me please!" he heard from outside.

"Red?" he wondered. He got up and went outside to see just who was getting beaten. He watched as some cocky young vamp lifted a woman off the ground. As soon as Edric saw the red hair, angry heat coursed through his body and he went into action. He leaped over the fence effortlessly, but not before the light haired pretty boy got another lick in. Thea's sobbing plea for someone to help her was almost more than his ancient heart could take and he tackled the other vampire.

"What the–?" The boy vampire was knocked on his ass just as he was closing in for his kill. He got himself up and was face to face with another vampire. "What's the deal man? I saw her first, she's mine," he yelled at Edric.

Thea hung on to consciousness. She blinked the blood out of her eyes and watched as Edric tackled her attacker. Good, she thought. That vampire had no idea what he had just gotten himself into. Relief spread through her and she allowed the darkness that she had been fighting, to take her over.

"Sorry, mate," Edric said. "But she belongs to me." Edric

recognized the boy from the photos Thea had given him. Another teenage vampire with no sire to teach him the ways. Edric grew more furious. He easily blocked three punches from the other vampire and caught the fourth punch in his fist. "Fine," Edric morphed into his dark side. "Have it your way."

The fight was brief, the new vamp was no match for the strength and power of Edric's demon. He threw the boy onto a broken tree branch and he exploded into flames and dust. "Stupid fledgling, no finesse." He kicked the pile of dust and tucked his demon away before walking toward Thea. "You all right, Red?" She didn't respond, but lay there limp on the ground. "Bloody hell." Edric knelt over her. "Thea? Forsythea?" No response, but still breathing. He lifted her into his arms, closing his eyes as the sweet smell of her blood called to him, remembering how she had tasted.

Edric carried Thea into his home and lay her on his bed. He felt her pulse: strong and steady. That was good. Not that he usually cared whether humans lived or died, as long as their killers kept things quiet for the rest of his Community, but this particular human he felt such a strong connection to. If anyone was going to kill her it was going to be him, and then only to turn her for himself.

Edric got up and retrieved some cloth to dress her wounds. The left side of her cheek was badly bruised, but the only cut was above her eyebrow. He fought to suppress his demon as he watched her blood seep from the small opening. He reached over and wiped some of the red ambrosia from her head and brought his fingers to his mouth. Damn, she tasted good. Edric felt an unusual sense of guilt creep over him and he began to clean Thea's lesion. He let his eyes wander down her body and noticed a scratch on her shoulder from where the vamp had torn her shirt. Bloody bastard, he thought, I should have tortured him some more.

Chapter 4

Thea slowly began to come around. She had a vague idea of where she was... on a bed at least... and still alive. She blinked a couple of times and then closed her eyes again. "Thea?" she heard from a million miles away, "Thea, time to wake up, Luv."

"Hmmm?" she stirred, "Edric?" She blinked up at the handsome vampire. She mumbled something as she closed her eyes again.

"Oh no you don't. Forsythea, wake up now."

"Hmmm? Wha..." Thea tried to sit up quickly but Edric's strong hands guided her head back down to the pillow.

"There now, Luv, easy does it. You've taken quite a blow." Edric was relieved, it's about time she woke up.

"What happened?" Thea brought her hand up to her head. She winced in pain as she probed the bandage. "Easy there, Luv, you don't want to start that bleeding again. Edric could smell the blood on the bandage but knew that it wasn't fresh. It had stopped over half an hour ago. It hadn't been deep, just bloody.

"I... I was bleeding?" Thea stared at Edric thoughtfully. She had to ask, "did you... you know... taste it?"

Edric looked directly in her eyes. "Yes," he said.

"Oh." Thea looked away. She didn't know if she minded or not. She didn't know what she was feeling right now. She felt like she was in some other world entirely.

"Forsythea," Edric began.

"No, it's okay. I mean, you're a ... and whatever. It's fine, really." She sat up, feeling much better now. She looked around. "You live here?" She didn't bother waiting for a response, of course he lived here. "Wow, nice place." Edric surrounded himself with deep shades of blues and greens. The bedroom had antique furniture and heavy drapery across what she assumed were the windows underneath. She could see a glimpse of the living area through the doorway and what she saw was also decorated in antiques and artwork. Not what she would have thought at all.

Edric let his eyes wander over his surroundings and then back at the beauty sitting up in his bed. "Now that you're awake," he began sternly, "you want to tell me just what the devil you were doing out at night all alone? You know what's out there now, Red, you've got to be more careful."

"My watch broke, I thought I had at least another half hour before sunset. I didn't realize how dark it was until I was halfway back to the car. I mean, it's not like I haven't ever gone out at night before. It's just that now suddenly there's all these... bad things out there. And I really don't know anybody around here and at least back home I had people to go out with and I always felt safe..." Thea finally looked up at Edric, tears threatening to fill those green orbs.

The helpless look in her eyes was enough to send Edric over the edge. It had been too long since he'd had a woman, and nearly a century since he had taken a human woman into his bed. He remembered their heat, their passion and their innocence. And this one was full of innocence just begging to be shattered. Edric leaned in closer to Thea, holding her eye contact. "You don't need any of them to feel safe, Pet." he said softly as he closed the distance between them. "I can make you feel safe, if you'll let me." He was so close he could taste her breath, smell her fear, and her arousal.

"Let you?" Thea said, hypnotized by his very presence.

"Will you let me?" Edric whispered as he brushed his lips across hers. He could hear her heart pounding beneath her flesh.

"Yes," Thea softly consented as she closed her eyes.

Edric could hardly contain himself as he waited for her to respond to his proposition. But this was all part of the fun, part of the seduction, the finesse. As soon as he heard her say yes his lips were upon hers, first gently and then with more force as he felt her respond to him. She was full of passion waiting to be let out.

Thea was breathless. Edric ignited in her a fire she hadn't even known she possessed. It felt so good, so dangerous, so passionate. She loved being seduced. She finally broke their kiss and gasped for air as he trailed her with kisses first across her jawline and then down her throat, pausing at her pulse points. She shivered in response, stiffening in anticipation of a bite.

Edric stopped, looked directly into her eyes and said, "Don't worry, Luv, I promise not to hurt you. Just trust me."

"I trust you," she said softly, " it's just that ...this whole thing is just a little... frightening..."

"I know, but I will never hurt you." He brushed her hair away from her ear and smiled, then became serious, "you don't ever have to pretend with me, Pet. You can be anything you ever wanted to be, do anything you ever wanted to do." He began raining kisses down her face to her throat once again. "I can teach you everything you ever wanted to know. I can show you more pleasures than you even knew existed," he purred.

Thea let the last of her resolve melt away as she let her desires take over the night. She felt Edric begin to unbutton her blouse. His lips followed his hands and she ran her fingers through his black hair. He unfastened her bra with expertise, tossing it and her blouse aside. Thea arched against him, encouraging him as he moved along her body. Wanting more contact with him she quickly tugged at his black t-shirt, pulling it out of his jeans.

Edric sat up, straddling her hips as he removed the shirt. Thea took in the smoothness of his broad chest. Edric let his head fall back as she ran her fingers first across his pecs, and then down his muscular six-pack, the heat of Thea's touch soaring through him, spreading like wild fire. His demon stirred within him in response. He had wanted her for so long.

A coy smile crossed Thea's lips as she let her fingers wander lower until they reached his leather belt. She paused, suddenly unsure of herself. "Go ahead, Luv." Edric looked at her with such desire in his eyes that an exciting chill ran up Thea's spine and then down to her toes. She unbuckled the belt.

Edric was having a very difficult time containing himself. Her very innocence aroused him deeper. He felt her fingers burn a trail across his chest and down his abdomen. He thought he was going to explode when she hesitated at his belt. As she unbuckled the leather strap he realized it had indeed been too long since he'd had a night quite like this one.

Thea reached for the top button of Edric's jeans and gasped when he suddenly grabbed her wrist. "Wait," he said as he slid further down the bed, "you first, Luv." He slowly peeled her tight jeans off of her, revealing white lace panties. "My god, you look good in lace." As he climbed back up the bed to her thighs, he felt Thea tremble, her slight fear feeding his demon. He began to rain kisses on the inside of her knee, paying special attention to the pit of the knee and its hidden erogenous zone.

Thea moaned in response and opened her knees more as she bent them. "Edric..." she breathed. Her hands found their way once more to his hair as he began his lips' journey up her thigh and Thea shivered in anticipation.

Edric could smell her arousal, his heightened vampire senses picking up the slightest changes in her body; allowing him to react to them perfectly. He led a trail of kisses up her thigh to the edge of her panties. He inhaled her scent and, biting the top of the lace, slowly pulled them off of her. She responded by lifting herself off the bed to ease the way. Edric smiled as he felt her grip on his hair tighten. He doubted anybody had ever given her this much pleasure before as he felt her muscles tensing beneath him. He glanced up at her and smiled. Her eyes were closed and her breasts shone with a covering of sweat.

Edric climbed up the bed and kissed Thea roughly, his

tongue penetrating into her mouth briefly. "I can't wait any longer, Pet," he breathed into her ear.

"Edric," Thea panted, "I want you inside me."

Edric slowly entered her hot, tight passage, allowing her time to adjust to his size before pulling out and thrusting back in again. He let out a loud moan as he found a quickening pace. Her heat felt like it would burn him.

Thea felt him enter her and thought for a moment she would tear. He felt so much bigger than any other lover. But then he allowed her muscles to adjust and soon she no longer felt discomfort, only pleasure. She moved in time with his thrusts and wondered how he could hold onto his control for so long. Edric's pace sped up and she could feel the tension in him build. He screamed her name as he filled her with his cold seed. Thea came immediately after, her legs tightening their hold around his waist. She held onto him until the waves of her powerful orgasm faded.

Edric waited until he felt her aftershocks subside before pulling out. He looked down at her face and couldn't help a small smile.

"What's so funny?" Thea asked.

"Nothing, Luv." He kissed her softly. "It's just been a long time since I've been with someone so...warm." He kissed her neck and whispered, "it feels so good. *You* feel so good." Edric had made a point to master the art of controlling the demon that dwelled inside of him. But it was difficult to be with her like this and not allow his demon its due. He didn't need to turn her, just taste her, mark her as his for all of the Community to know. The mark would protect her; but he knew right now biting her would drive her away. *He* wanted her, not just to satisfy the beast within, but to satisfy his fleeting humanity.

Thea moaned under him and tilted her head to one side, granting him access to her neck. Seeing her stretched out throat like that tested Edric's resolve to keep his promise to her. She didn't even realize how she was torturing him with her actions. After he was sure she was asleep tonight, he would have to go hunting. No amount of bagged blood will feed this craving.

She took a deep breath, "my god, Edric, you make me feel... alive."

"Do I?" Edric laughed evilly. "Enjoyed that, did you, my Pet?" He rolled them over so that Thea was on top and captured her mouth in a gentle kiss. "Well, there's more in store if you'll let me show you. But first we rest a bit." He tightened his embrace and waited for her to fade off to sleep.

Thea closed her eyes, feeling safe and not alone for the first time in months. She lay atop Edric's cool body and drifted off into a peaceful slumber.

*****

Edric waited a good forty-five minutes before he trusted that Thea was deeply asleep enough for him to sneak out from under her delicate weight. Without a sound he got dressed and slipped out for the night, remembering to actually lock the door this time. He usually had no reason to use any kind of security for himself. He feared no vampire nor any other creature, and if any human dared to try to break in he would simply hunt them down and kill them. Somehow the rest of the world, underworld included, seemed to know this. But with Thea inside, he would rather she be safe.

He parked his car in the parking lot of *Nightly's,* but instead of going inside he decided to take a walk further into downtown. He didn't just want a meal, he wanted to hunt. He owed it to the darker side of himself to have a little fun after the romp he had just had *without* feeding from Thea. He knew where the gangs hung out. Hopefully they were up for some fun.

It didn't take long for him to stumble upon a group of three Hispanic men with bandanas around their foreheads. Edric stuffed the tips of his fingers into the front pockets of his denim pants, hunched his shoulders up and put his head down, looking as if he were trying to disappear. The bait was set.

One of the gang members started walking next to him. "Hey, man, nice jacket. Yo, I need a leather jacket like that."

Another member started walking on the other side of Edric. "You know, Francisco, I bet this guy would give you *his* jacket, man."

Edric slowed down and shook his head. "I don't want any trouble, mate."

"Hear that, Luis?" said Francisco. "He *wants* to give me his jacket."

Edric stopped moving forward when he finally saw that the third man had found his way to blocking his path. He hid his satisfaction well.

"Hey, Claudio, this guy wants to give his jacket to Francisco," Luis commented.

Claudio and the others just laughed. Edric put on his most convincing face as he put his hands slightly out in front of him. "Now, hold on, mate. I said I didn't want any trouble; I didn't say I was going to give you my jacket."

"Wait a minute," said Luis mockingly. "You mean you *lied* to us?"

The trio slowly began to enclose themselves upon what they thought was their prey. "I don't like being lied to, man." Francisco pulled out a switch blade and the sound of it springing to life excited Edric. Now it was getting interesting.

Luis and Claudio pulled their own knives, and they all had evil grins on their pathetic faces.

Edric took three steps back. "Okay, okay, you're right, I did lie," he admitted, stopping the would-be attackers where they stood. "I actually *did* come looking for trouble."

Edric was naturally faster, or rather, unnaturally faster, than humans, but he tried not to use this advantage, in order to keep the encounter from being over too soon. Their positions, skill level and possible attacks were already calculated before the assault began. Francisco came at him first, from the right.

Edric stepped into him, striking the attacker's right leg with a stunning kick to take away his balance. He simultaneously controlled Francisco's right hand with his left, and backfisted him in the face with his right. Immediately, he followed up with a thrust kick to the left leg, snapping it audibly at the knee.

The scream of excruciation was delicious and Edric was thrilled to see Claudio ready to comply with an attack of his own. When the gang member lunged forward with his knife, Edric easily dodged it by moving into and to the outside of Claudio's arm. Edric tore at the flesh of the forearm, drawing blood as he ripped through the muscle, and left four deep gashes from his demonic claws. He lifted the arm and tore at the man's ribcage, before tossing the doubled over body toward the remaining human.

Luis stood there, mouth agape in shock. "Your eyes..." is all he managed before dropping the box cutter he was holding and turning to run for his life.

"Oh, Luis," Edric said to himself. "Didn't anyone ever tell you to never run from a wild beast? It attracts their attention." He inhaled deeply, picking up the scent of fear and sweat, and took off after him, leaving the two wounded men to survive. After all, how much could he really eat in one night anyway.

In a state of panic, Luis ran for cover into an abandoned warehouse and hid behind a stack of wooden pallets to catch his breath. After a few seconds he breathed a sigh of relief at the thought that the crazy red-eyed man hadn't been able to follow him.

"Luis...?" a sinister voice sang out into the darkness. Luis held his breath, trying to figure out just where the bastard was. He started to quietly crawl in the dark toward the back of the building from his hiding spot, and froze when he heard a thump that sounded like someone had jumped up onto the pile of pallets he had only just left moments before. As silently as he could, he got himself to an old canvas tarp and crawled under it.

"I'll bet," the voice continued, "that you're wondering what it is that you just saw, aren't you, Luis?" The man under the canvas sat perfectly still, barely even breathing; he had hidden for the safety of his life more than once and escaped. This was no different.

"I'll bet you're thinking, were that guy's eyes really red?" Edric jumped off of the pallets and walked around slowly, enjoying the game. "Well, Luis, my eyes glow red when the demon inside of me comes to the surface." He took his time as he walked around near the canvas that he saw the pitiful human crawl under, like a cockroach running for cover from the light.

Luis found himself listening very carefully to what the lunatic was saying. Demon? What the hell was he talking about? But, then again, his eyes *were* red. He heard and felt the guy pass right by him and started to allow himself to breathe again. He continued to listen intently, waiting for him to get far enough away so Luis could sneak out safely.

"My demon *loves* to hunt, Luis. It loves the fight, the chase, and it especially loves the reward after the bait and trap."

The voice sounded like it was moving away and Luis started to relax a little. But then the canvas flew off of him, and he stared, wide-eyed, into those orbs of blood. And that face, those teeth. "Dios mio." he managed.

"And it *loves* to eat."

*****

Just about a half hour later, Edric passed by the sight of the knife fight, that the surviving members of Luis's gang had tried to pull off. He could smell the leftover odor of blood as he passed where Claudio had stood when Edric had slashed his arm and ribcage. For a moment he wondered if the gang, whatever the name of it was, would try to track him down and deal out punishment. He smiled at the thought. Now *that* would be fun.

It wasn't long before he entered *Nightly's,* his home away from home. The place where, at one time or another, every vampire in the area eventually strolled into each night, where he could see his children and his community. He kept it small, intimate, knowing full well that too many demons in one area would attract too much attention. There were rules, and there were punishments.

"Edric!" The bartender greeted him with a smile. The only vampire around who was older than he; the original Salty Dog if ever there was one.

"'Ello, Cap'n." Edric sat at the bar and took the offered drink from the old barkeep.

"You're looking mighty satisfied, Edric. Anything good out there tonight?"

Edric smiled and held up his glass to the other vampire. "To good hunting, Cap'n," he said.

Captain held up his own drink. "Aye," he agreed." Once they had emptied their glasses and refilled them, Captain said in a lowered voice, "people are talking about the pretty redhead that came calling for you, Edric. New source?"

Edric went solemn. "No, not a source, old friend." He looked down at his drink for a moment.

"Oh no," Captain said, shaking head head slowly. "This isn't good, y'know. These kinda things with humans never end well; I don't have to tell you that."

"This one's different," Edric defended quietly.

"No, she's not. Mark her or turn her, Edric; but don't try and have some kinda relationship with her." Captain let his advice set in, then he added, "does she even know what you are?"

Edric drained his glass and slid it across to the bartender. "Yes; and I don't bloody well remember asking you for your input, old man." He threw a few dollars on the bar and got up to leave.

"Edric, wait." Captain said. "I'm sorry, didn't mean nuthin' by it. Just trying to protect you, is all."

Edric turned to him with a half smile of forgiveness. "It's been a long time since I've needed your help, Cap'n."

Edric walked over to a nearby table and put his hand on the shoulder of the larger of the two men sitting there. "Liam," he said. "I have a job for you."

*****

It was almost four o'clock in the morning when Edric entered his house, quietly, so as not to disturb his sleeping prize. It was an earlier night than usual for him, but he wanted to lay beside Thea some more before she woke up. Who knew what kind of questions he would have to field when she did. He wanted to enjoy lying there beside her, and fall asleep to the rhythm of her heartbeat.

Chapter 5

It was difficult to tell whether Edric was asleep or not since he didn't actually breathe, an eerie fact, Thea discovered. But after lying there awake for about fifteen minutes after she woke up, she felt that his grip around her had loosened enough to indicate sleep, and she was able to wriggle out of his arms without disturbing him. She wondered what time he had come back last night. Sure enough she had woken up around midnight or so, to find an empty bed. At first she was a little hurt but then she thought about it and it had made some sense. She had been exhausted and had simply rolled over and gone back to sleep.

She grabbed her clothes from the floor, but when she held up her torn blouse, she decided to grab Edric's shirt instead, and headed down the hall for a much needed shower. She found fresh black towels in the linen closet next to the bathroom.

She stood under the steaming water until her finger tips wrinkled, and she thought about leaving. She had so many questions, but she was afraid once she left, she might never have the opportunity to know the answers again. She exited the shower and got dressed before realizing that there was no mirror in the bathroom. Well, that answers one question, she thought.

She got her make-up out of her satchel and checked herself in the compact mirror. She frowned at the bruises on her cheek and wondered how she would ever explain them to anyone. She couldn't very well say that she was attacked by a blood-sucking creature of the night. Another mugging? She sighed heavily and put away the make-up.

Three times she had nearly gotten killed and all three times Edric had been there to save her. Had he been stalking her? Watching out for her the whole time, knowing what evils live out there in the darkness? And why haven't all these people who are being turned into vampires shown up in the obituaries? Why hasn't anyone in town noticed these missing people? She finished getting dressed and took a better look around Edric's home.

It was a small, but spacious two bedroom home, the other bedroom set up as a small library. Antique furniture was in every room, yet the decor was still somewhat contemporary. There were few, if any, electronics and every window was covered by heavy draperies. She pushed one aside and looked out into the park. The sun was brightly shining and there were teenagers along the fence line again. She looked but did not see Mr. David Francis Arthur, and she wondered exactly what part he played in all of this.

The kitchen had stainless steel appliances and she was at first horrified, but then a little relieved to find small bags of blood in the refrigerator. At least she knew that he didn't always hunt for his meals. She shook her head and wondered, not for the first time, what the hell she had gotten herself into.

To be honest, she was a little afraid to just leave before Edric got up. She wondered if he would sleep all day. She wasn't even sure what time it was. She rummaged through her bag but knew her cell phone was not in there. She always attached it to her jeans and since it wasn't around then it must have fallen off while she was being attacked in the park. Dare she go look for it? It had all her contacts in there, and she foolishly had never written any down on actual paper. She wondered if she could sneak out, find her phone and a bite to eat, and come back before Edric woke up. There was nothing she could eat in any of the cabinets so she would need to go out eventually. She hated the thought of anyone seeing her right now, though. She fought the urge to run away and decided instead to do some reading.

Quietly she unpacked the library book from her satchel, mentally thanking Edric for bringing it along. She curled up on the soft leather couch and began reading *Vampires & Folklore*, hoping to find some answers.

*****

It was dusk when Edric finally awoke, and he wasn't all that surprised to find that Thea had left the bed. He found her on the couch reading a ridiculous book on vampire myths. She looked up when he entered the living room and watched him as he joined her on the couch. He quietly removed the book from her hands and laid it on the antique coffee table. He searched her eyes, knowing they held many questions. "Go ahead," he invited, "ask me. What do you want to know?"

"Anything?"

"Yes."

"And you'll tell me the truth."

"I have never lied to you, Thea, I won't start now."

Thea took a breath and decided to go with general information first. "Are vampires immortal?"

"Basically, yes."

"How can they be killed?"

"Wood through the heart, fire, decapitation or a bit too much sun."

"What about crosses and holy water?"

Edric slowly shook his head no, his eyes captivating hers, never letting them waver for a second.

"I saw you out in the sunlight the other day, I don't understand, how is that possible?" Thea stayed on the opposite end of the sofa from him and she was thankful that he hadn't moved toward her. She wanted all of her questions answered before anymore physical contact, knowing how easily he could control her body once she allowed him access to her.

"It was overcast, I was in the shade of a tree and we can go out in the day as long as we have just fed. Feeding helps to heal us."

Thea thought about his answer as she mentally searched through what she had seen in the book. "The book says you have to be invited to enter someone's home?"

"Yes, but anyone in the home can do it, doesn't need to be the owner." He wondered if she would ever invite him into her apartment. Maybe, in time. He could see the torment she was putting herself through as she tried to come to grips with the truth. "Anything else?"

"Is it true that a person can be turned by a certain number of bites and then three days later they wake up as a vampire?"

"No." He hoped that would be enough but knew it wouldn't be. He didn't want to tell her the process of turning someone.

"Then how?"

"Forsythea, you don't want to know this."

"Yes, I do. I need to know how this happens, please, just tell me."

Edric sighed. "A human would be drained nearly dry. Then the sire would cut himself and have the childe drink his blood. They wake up within ten or twelve hours, hungry. Without the sire there to help them through the first few weeks their demons can take over, ripping through towns on a bloodthirsty rampage."

"Have you ever turned anyone?"

"Forsythea..."

"Have you ever turned anyone?" She closed her eyes when she asked the second time, unable to look at him, knowing the answer.

"I have been a vampire for 126 years, Red, I have turned many. But I have always taught them to be..." He stopped, knowing nothing he could say would make it sound nice. "I haven't sired in many years."

Thea was silent for a few moments, but by no means done. "The girl that bit me and the kid last night..."

"No sire is teaching them. Someone's turning children, Thea, and I need to find out who it is and stop them. You don't turn children."

"What? There's a rule book?" She was growing agitated.

"Unwritten, but yeah, there are rules, *I* have rules."

"Like what? Or is it members only?"

Edric's eyes narrowed at her attitude. She must have sensed this and looked away. She was having a more difficult time with this than he would have thought. He got up and knelt down before her, noticing the tears building in her eyes. Gently he touched her face and brushed his thumb over her lips as they quivered. "This is crazy," she whispered. "Am I going crazy?"

Tears began streaming down her cheeks and Edric felt an ache in his still heart. He got up and sat next to her, pulling her into his arms.

She leaned against him and held onto him for dear life, for sanity's sake. This could not be happening. Why is it that the only time she felt safe and secure was in the arms of this man?

This man, who wasn't a man at all, but was a thing you only ever read about and saw in horror movies. And what about him? What were his plans? Did he plan on turning her into this childe he spoke of? She was so confused. What was he, valiant savior or evil demon? "What will become of me?" she asked into his chest.

He looked at her confused. "What? What do you mean?" Realization dawned on him after searching her eyes and he hugged her fiercely. "Oh, Thea." He broke their embrace and lifted her head so that she looked at him. "Look at me. I will *never* hurt you. I will never do anything you don't want me to do. I swear to you." He hugged her again and kissed the top of her head.

Had she thought that was what he had planned all along? He could imagine her sitting here waiting to see if it would come to pass, a nightmare, she would be sure. Yet she had stayed, had not left given the opportunity. He felt her calming down and let her move herself out of his arms. She wouldn't look at him. He remembered why it had been so long since he had taken a human lover; so many emotions. Most vampires were lust and desire and anger, that's all, it took years for them to regain their humanity, and only those who wanted to.

Thea took a moment to get a hold of her confused emotions. She believed Edric when he told her he would never hurt her. He had never lied to her yet, and had only proven to be strong and dependable. Her thoughts went back to what he had said before. "These children being turned, you think the old man in the park has something to do with it?"

"Yes." Edric was glad to be off the topic of what makes a vampire a vampire, and back onto something that he was determined to put an end to. "I think his son is a vampire and that this David Arthur character is bringing him his food. He's being careful to pick only children who are junkies, who have either already left home or have been taken from their homes by Child Protective Services."

Thea nodded thoughtfully. "How can I help?"

"I'm not sure you can, Luv. I have to go over there and take care of this vampire." He left out the part about probably having to take care of the old man too.

"I'll come with you."

"You bloody well will not!" Edric said sternly, his drawl becoming thicker with his ire.

"Why not?" she raised her voice.

"Are you bleedin' daft?" he yelled, getting up to pace the floor in front of her, furious at the thought. "You will stay away from that house at all costs. I can't promise to be able to protect you there."

"Why not? You must be more powerful than he is. You're a hundred years older."

"No, and that's final." He stopped and looked at her. "Why would you want to go anyhow?"

Thea stood to face him. "Because I don't want you to kill the old man."

Edric tightened his jaw, careful not to say something that could ruin everything. He grabbed her gently by the arms. "Forsythea, that old man is responsible for at least nine or ten children's lives so far. And he's going to keep on doing what he's doing because he thinks that monster in his house is still his son, and it's not. Eventually, he will become just as dead as the children he is feeding to his boy."

He led her to sit down on the couch again. "This vampire isn't playing by the rules, Thea. He won't leave you alone just because he smells a master vampire on you. He'll take you and kill you and turn you, and god only knows what else he'll do for fun before that. I won't be able to do what I need to do if I'm worried about where you are and if you're alive or dead, or worse." He cupped her face once again. "Forsythea, promise me you will not go looking for this man."

She nodded her oath and Edric kissed her gently before leaning back on the couch, taking her with him.

She leaned against his chest, exhausted from everything she had absorbed in the past twenty-four hours. She wanted nothing more than to sleep away this nightmare. She had so many other questions for Edric but her head hurt and she didn't think she could take anymore. She was starving, not having eaten anything all day. The growling of her stomach made this quite obvious.

"You need to eat," Edric stated. "How about we go get something for you?"

Thea shook her head. "No, I don't want to go out there right now."

He smiled. "You'll be safe with me, Thea."

"I don't doubt that at all. Even so, I don't need to go showing off my bruises right now. Can't we just order in?"

"Anything you want," he answered. "But I don't have a phone, so you'll have to use yours."

Thea sighed in frustration. "Can't; I must have dropped it last night at some point while I was running for my life through the park."

Edric got up from the couch and went into the bedroom. He emerged a moment later holding her phone. "You're right, you did; but I grabbed it before I brought you here."

Thea was thrilled. She jumped off the couch and took her cell. It was almost out of power but there was enough left to call in for a pizza.

*****

Three hours later, Edric sat there on the couch with Thea in his arms until he was certain she had fallen asleep. He eased her head down onto the cushion and covered her with a blanket. Normally, he did not use the heat in the house all that much, but he turned it up a notch before slipping out the door. There was business to attend to.

*****

When Thea woke up she noticed immediately that she was alone. She folded the blanket that Edric had apparently covered her with and looked around. She wondered how it was that Edric could afford such a nice place right off Main Street in the village. Add that one to the list of many questions to ask, along with pretty much every detail about his century old life and... before. She replaced the library book back into her satchel. That will go back first thing in the morning.

She went into the small kitchen and noticed a piece of paper lying on the counter with her keys on top of it. She placed her keys into her pants pocket and read the note.

Your car is in the driveway.

Don't worry, you'll be safe.

Will contact you as soon as I can.

~ Edric

Thea folded up the note and put it in her back pocket before gathering her things, and headed for the door. She hesitated with her hand on the knob; it was dark out already, and she thought it was pretty late at that. *Don't worry, you'll be safe* the note had read. Slowly she turned the knob and peered out the door. Her car was indeed right there in the driveway, just a few short feet away. She was terrified to go out there but was anxious to get back into her own home where she hadn't invited anyone, except for Josh, and she was fairly certain that he was as human as they came.

Holding the keys in her trembling fingers she aimed them at the car and pressed the unlock button on her key chain. Gripping the stake in her hand from her coat pocket she ran to the car and jumped in, locking the doors immediately. She started the car and drove the brief four miles out of the village and into the lot of her apartment complex.

She circled around three times before giving up on getting a spot right up close to the door. She parked the car and took a deep breath before venturing out of the vehicle, keys in one hand and the other inside her pocket, holding onto her stake. She looked around her nervously before briskly walking toward the entrance to her building.

Her heart jumped into her throat when a man stepped out in front of her as she approached the door. He was tall and broad. His sandy hair fell to his shoulders and his blue eyes were just as intense as Edric's. Small chains hung from his leather jacket in various places. She recognized him at once. "Liam," she gasped.

"Just making sure you get home safe and sound," he said stepping out from the shadows.

Thea took a step back, not letting him any closer. "Edric?"

Liam nodded once. "Told me to make sure you got home without incident."

"Where is he?" She thought she knew, but asked anyway.

"Out taking care of some business. Edric said you have a knack for getting into trouble, told me I was to keep you safe."

Thea didn't necessarily trust him, but Edric did. Remembering his interaction with him at the bar, she wondered if Edric was Liam's sire. "Please do not stand between me and my door," she said.

Liam complied and watched her open the door to the building and step across the threshold. He seemed satisfied and turned to leave.

"Liam?" she said quietly. "Thank you."

He nodded and walked into the darkness.

Chapter 6

Regardless of how late it had become, the first thing Thea did when she got home was to draw a hot bath. She added plenty of bubbles to it and checked her bruises in her bathroom mirror. Her cheek was worse than it had seemed in her small compact make-up mirror. She tenderly touched the purple blotch on her cheekbone and was surprised when it didn't hurt that badly. Clearly, it was not as bad as it looked. She was thankful just to have survived the assault.

Soaking in a hot bath, Thea closed her eyes and let her thoughts settle. She had never felt such a hurricane of emotions. Terror at being attacked, relief that Edric had saved her, immense pleasure at his touch, and absolute confusion as she tried to put her thoughts around all of it being real. But what was the most disturbing was the undeniable fact that she enjoyed the rush of excitement surrounding the whole thing.

She had to wonder if she should ever see Edric again. If it

was up to her heart, she would be with him right now, finding out what was going on in the Arthur household. It was the emerging investigator within her. But the more grounded part of her wanted to never look into this dark world she had just gotten a peek at. There was no denying what Edric was; she had easily accepted, once over the initial shock of it, that vampires existed, and that Edric was one of them. He made her feel real for once in her life, like she had a purpose. She just needed to learn to deal with the terrorizing part of it, and now that she knew what lie in the darkness outside, could she ever really feel safe *without* him by her side?

She sighed and placed the washcloth over her eyes. She let her mind wander to the old man and his son. What had happened, she wondered. Had Mr. Arthur found his son, brought him home and before he had time to call anyone, had the son risen? Right in front of his father?

She imagined Mr. Arthur being trapped by his son, or whatever he was now, no longer a father but a slave to the demon his son had become, holding onto the hope that someday his boy would come back to him. Now he was forced to bring him someone to feed from on a regular basis, like some kind of sick Renfield character. How often? Weekly? Daily?

Wait a minute, Thea sat up in the tub, how often? Do they eat as regularly as humans do? She thought back to the contents of Edric's refrigerator where there were dozens of bags of blood. They must eat at least once a day. So why was it that there were only children missing once a week? Why was it Mr. Arthur only needed to go to the park on Saturdays? What did his son eat in between? Thea exited her bath and quickly got dressed. What if Mr. Arthur went to different places each day to bring unsuspecting victims to his son, and the few children that Edric had... taken care of, were just the few that got out? There could be an army of... what? Minions? What if what Edric had walked into was nothing less than a hive of demons?

Thea turned on her laptop and rummaged through the information she had gathered for Edric. She hadn't paid all that much attention to the son's death; what was his name? Patrick, she thought as she more carefully reread the article written by the

Chronicle on the disappearance of a local wealthy heir. There wasn't much information, as Mr. Arthur conveniently made himself unavailable for comment. Only that the twenty-two year old was presumed dead after being in a boating accident, his body was never found., but his boat washed ashore about a week after he initially went out. Thea sat back in her chair. Of course his body was never found, it was still sitting in his own home.

Thea found herself worrying about Edric. Like it or not, whatever he was, she had gotten her heart involved with this man and couldn't help the feelings that had already developed. The question of whether or not she should see him again was nonsense. If she should or shouldn't, it made no difference because she knew in her heart that she would. She wondered if there was anything she could do. Whatever mess Edric had gotten himself into, would he really need help from her? Thea got up and grabbed her satchel, she had to do something and she thought she knew someone who might help.

*****

It was well after midnight when Thea pulled into the parking lot of the pub and waited. She hoped she wouldn't need to go inside, but after waiting there anxiously for the longest ten minutes of her life, she opened her door. She gave a small scream when it quickly closed right back on her.

"Edric's right," Liam said when she rolled down her window. "You do have a knack for getting into trouble."

Thea got control of herself as best she could before speaking, "Liam, have you heard from Edric yet?"

"No, he's taking care of business."

"Don't you think he should have been back by now? He might be in trouble."

Liam laughed, "believe me, Edric can take care of himself." He turned to leave.

Thea jumped out of her car. "Wait! Can I ask you a question?"

Liam opened his arms. "Ask away."

Thea cleared her throat nervously. "How often does a..., do you need to feed?"

Liam cocked an eyebrow and walked the short distance between them. "I'm a little hungry right now, Missy, you offering?"

Thea tried to forced her heart to stay steady, but doubted she was very successful. When the hell did she become so excited by danger and bad boys? "I don't think Edric would like that, do you?" She was playing the sire card.

Liam's eyes narrowed.

"Please; it's important."

"We like to eat as often as anyone else, at least every day. Why?"

"I think that there are more vampires in that house than Edric thought."

"So what?"

"Aren't you concerned? It's been hours," she pleaded with him.

"Concern is a human emotion." Liam completely closed the distance between them and Thea found herself pressing up against her car her as he spoke. "Never forget what we are, no matter how much Edric tries to hold onto his humanity, it doesn't change *what* we are." He stared at her for a few seconds and then headed back to the pub.

"I'm going to find him!" Thea yelled after him. "And you promised to keep me safe, so be prepared; if he's not home by tomorrow night, I'm going to the Hills." Liam didn't turn around but Thea thought she saw him stiffen at her words. Tomorrow was Saturday, and Mr. Arthur should be at the park.

*****

Thea was up early, or rather she hadn't actually slept much after her meeting with Liam. She dressed in comfortable clothes and grabbed her coat before heading to the park. But first a quick stop at Edric's house, just to make sure he hadn't come home. She knew almost immediately that the house would be empty. She couldn't explain it, but she was indeed correct. Not a thing had been moved since she had left there the night before; and it was uncomfortably warm. She took the time to lower the thermostat before heading to her next stop.

She waited in her car across from the park for over an hour and nothing had happened. Maybe this was good news, she thought to herself. If Mr. Arthur didn't show up then she could assume that Edric did what he had to do, so there was no reason for the old man to come choose another victim. But if that were the case, why hadn't Edric come home yet? No, more likely that Mr. Arthur was no longer among the living; he was either dead or undead.

It was around eleven o'clock when Mr. Arthur finally showed up and sat in the same bench she had seen him in the week before. Thea had been right to worry; something had obviously gone very wrong.

She pinned her press badge to her lapel, and proceeded to walk over to him. "Mr. Arthur?" she smiled.

He looked up at her. "Yes?"

Thea extended her hand. "My name is Thea Daniels and I'm with the *Pellman Chronicle*, how do you do?"

He smiled, "fine, thank you." He gestured to the bench, "Won't you join me?"

"Actually, Mr. Arthur I don't have time right now, but we're doing a piece on the town's proposal for the beautification of downtown Pellman, and I would really like to get the opinion of someone of your stature in the community. I understand the Arthur family has been in Pellman for three generations."

"Yes, that's true," he responded.

"Well, I was wondering if you had time for an interview? Unfortunately, I have meetings all day, but perhaps you would have time maybe this evening?"

Mr. Arthur smiled slowly. "Yes," he agreed. "This evening would be just fine."

"Wonderful, thank you, Mr. Arthur; this really means a lot to me. Is seven o'clock all right with you?"

Mr. Arthur stood. "Very well, I will see you this evening." He looked at her. "I assume then, Miss Daniels, that you already know where I live?"

Thea smiled back. "Of course, Mr. Arthur."

"See you tonight then, my dear." He tipped his hat and

turned away from her.

Thea watched him get into his white Lincoln sedan and drive off. He had done exactly what Thea had thought he would do. Since she was coming over tonight, there would be no reason for him to coax another young victim to his home. Why should he, when one was so willing to come of her own accord?

Thea drove to Edric's home and let herself in, deciding to wait there, wanting to be closer to him. She contemplated what she had just set in motion and decided to pray, something she hadn't done since she was a child. She lay on the bed they had shared, and although she closed her eyes, she did not sleep.

At six-thirty she got up and went to Edric's refrigerator. She grabbed two small bags of blood, *it heals us,* and stuffed them into her coat pocket before heading for the door.

She arrived at the address in The Hills by six-forty-five. She leaned up against her car parked across the street and waited. She was not disappointed. He came up and stood next to her. "Thank you for coming, Liam."

He glared at her. "Edric's not going to like this, Missy."

She ignored his comment. "Is he in there?"

Liam nodded.

"Is he alive? Hurt?"

"It's not a video camera we have between us."

She looked at him. "Then what is it, exactly?"

He shrugged. "A bond between sire and childe. I am bound to him, as I am to my word to him. If he's in trouble, I have to help him. Our demons are linked. Not a decision as much as an instinct."

"Are there others?"

"I sense only one other."

Thea looked back at the house. "I told the old man I wanted an interview with him. I think I should go in alone. Hopefully, I can steal away and find Edric and get out of there."

Liam stood face to face with Thea. "And what will you do when he goes and feeds you to his son?"

"Come up to the house with me, stand in the shadows, and once I enter I will whisper you an invitation before I close the door behind me."

"Thought of everything, have you?" he said, "I've got a better idea, after you invite me in I storm the castle and we get Edric and get the hell out right then and there."

"No. I'm trying to save the old man's life. He's a victim in this as much as all those children are. Give me thirty minutes, if I don't come out, then come in."

"If I feel the need to go in, then I'm going in, I don't care how much time has passed."

Thea nodded, knowing that it was as good as any agreement that she was going to get.

She walked up the long driveway somewhat alone, knowing Liam was somewhere in the darkness, *don't worry, you'll be safe.* She rang the bell and took deep breaths to calm her nerves. There was no going back now. Maybe she should just let Liam go in and get Edric. No, she couldn't, she knew the old man would get killed in the process. He was the final victim to save in all of this.

Inside the bowels of the house Edric's demon stirred. He stood up and let it search the area. Without thinking he took one step too many and passed through the darkened square that was his cell. The white hot light burned him and he hissed as he jumped back. He composed himself quickly. Forsythea had come for him, and so had Liam. He glanced over at the other vampire still sleeping. It would end soon.

*****

Thea followed Mr. Arthur into the sitting room. She had never in her life been in such a manor. Mr. Arthur motioned for her to sit. "Mr. Arthur..." she began.

"Please," he said as he poured some tea, "call me David."

Thea thanked him for the tea but didn't dare touch it, especially since David made no moves to drink his. She wasn't some foolish street kid and knew he must be drugging them . How else would an old man overpower a young man? "Okay then, David, I don't have a lot of time, so I'm going to get right to the point. I'm not here because of the beautification project."

*****

Outside Liam walked the perimeter of the large home, searching for the strongest pull of his sire. Finally he came to a place in the foundation that should have had a basement window, but instead a piece of steel had replaced the glass. He wondered if he could break through it; he thought he might if he allowed his demon full control over him, something he had never done, on Edric's order.

*****

David leaned back in his chair. "And what exactly *is* the point of your visit then, Miss Daniels?"

"Well," Thea cleared her throat, "I think I know what happened to your son, Patrick."

*****

Edric stood tall and waited. "What is it?" He heard the other vampire ask, "Is he coming?"

Edric looked at the younger vampire. He was sickly pale and had the look of a defeated and abused animal. "Not yet, Patrick.

But when he does you need to stand down, no matter *who* he brings down with him. Do you understand me?" Edric let his eyes turn crimson when he glared at Patrick, who winced at the more powerful demon.

*****

Thea needed to move quickly. "David, your son wasn't lost, was he? You found him and brought him home right here in this house. And then, like some miracle, he had come back to life, hadn't he?" Thea watched as the old man's face grew suddenly white, his mouth dropping ever so slightly. She continued, "He must have been very hungry. Who did he grab?"

David's vision blurred for a moment at the memory of that first night when he had found Patrick on the beach right outside their own back door. He looked away from the girl across from him. "The dog," he whispered.

Thea got up and sat next to David. She put a reassuring hand over his own. "I know he's been keeping you hostage here, making you bring him his victims to feed on."

David raised his head. "Yes."

"It's time to end this, David," Thea paused. "He's not your son anymore."

David looked at her then. "He's a monster," he said quietly.

*****

Liam found a tool shed in the back yard. He easily broke off the lock and found exactly what he was looking for. He grabbed the sledge hammer and walked back to the steel window.

*****

Edric watched Patrick pace, his demon's hunger getting the better of him. Edric didn't think the young vampire would be able to control his demon at all, once Thea was brought down. He would need to move very quickly. "Calm your demon, Patrick."

Patrick stopped and looked at Edric. "How? I'm so hungry I can't even think. I can smell someone is here, someone young... and female."

Edric saw Patrick's eyes turning shades of red as his demon got closer to the surface. "You will stand down, Patrick!"

*****

They were both quiet for a few moments. Then David stood and started to walk out of the room. "When I first found Patrick I thought he had drunk himself to death, fallen out of his boat and drowned."

Thea followed him into the kitchen. "That must have been horrible for you."

"It was. I don't know where I got the strength to drag his body into the house." David opened a door and began walking downstairs, never looking at Thea, always assuming she was right behind him. And she played the fool so well, she did not disappoint. "I found him at six-thirty in the morning when I went out for my run with the dog." He stopped at the bottom of the staircase and looked at Thea. "When he sat up the dog was just there and ... he grabbed her so quickly and just..."

Thea touched his arm sympathetically.

"I didn't know what to do. He seemed better after that, lucid, and I thought of all my research." He walked over to a steel door. "It's amazing what one could do with the right amount of light." He opened the door and ushered Thea inside.

She stopped dead at the sight before her. There stood Edric and another vampire, each occupying a 10x10 square of darkened area in a room otherwise drowning with hot lights. She looked over at Edric, horrified. He slowly moved his head to one side, signaling her to keep quiet. The other vampire was downright frightening. He was beyond pale and Thea could see he was already changing. He paced like a caged tiger, eyes darting from her to Edric and back to her again. "David, what have you done?"

"I have taken advantage of an opportunity to study an animal that up until now only existed in nightmares and novels. Did you know that crosses and holy water do nothing to them? But starve them enough and they cannot stand the heat of these lights."

Thea dared not take her eyes from the new vampire. Ever so slowly she began making her way so that she was more in front of Edric than Patrick. She knew there was no way David was letting her go. He had brought her down as a meal, and all she could do now was pray that her faith in Edric was not misplaced.

"I had just about grown bored with my new line of work when this one came to my door." He gestured to Edric. "Like a gift from God. I had no idea of what he was at first, but he drank the tea and when I brought him down here Patrick told me. Imagine what I would be able to learn with two creatures! How do they socialize? Will they fight each other for food or work cooperatively? Such possibilities!"

Thea looked at the old man, baffled at how easily she had been fooled. "David, I am begging you to stop this. You don't know what you're doing, you can't possibly think you can survive all of this."

"There are worse things than death, my dear." He put his hand on the handle of the door. "I'm sorry." He opened the door and stepped out.

Before Thea had a chance to get to Edric the lights went out, leaving only an eerie green glow by some low powered lights in each corner. Patrick immediately leaped at her. She closed her eyes and screamed.

Edric had carefully watched Patrick the whole time the old man had talked to Thea. The young demon was full of hunger, like a rabid wolf. Patrick had no control over his demon whatsoever, and would simply let it take over once the room went dark. He watched Thea slowly make her way closer to him, instinctively increasing the distance between herself and Patrick. Such a simple action, it most definitely saved her life.

Once the lights went out Patrick pounced. Edric flew to intercept. He heard Thea scream as he ran Patrick against the opposite wall from her. Slamming him against the steel wall Edric roared, "I said, stand down!"

Patrick kicked Edric in the stomach, sending him back. He ran at Edric's legs in a tackler's grab. Edric dropped his elbow onto Patrick's spine as soon as he felt arms around his legs. Patrick fell to the ground but bit into Edric's calf. Edric yelled in pain and kicked Patrick on the side of his face. Patrick rolled and looked up at Thea, Edric no longer between them.

"Edric!" Thea screamed, seeing the starvation in Patrick's face but stood frozen in terror. Above her a piece of the wall banged loudly once before falling to the floor in front of her. They all looked up as Liam dropped down from the window. He stood in front of Thea protectively and Patrick stopped just long enough for Edric to bring him down.

Edric grabbed Patrick in a bear hug and threw him to the ground. He stayed atop him, pinning him down and snarled, "you have a choice, Patrick, stop now and I will feed you, or go against me once more and die."

Patrick ceased his struggle. "So hungry..." he pleaded.

"I know," Edric said. "But I *will* kill you. I am losing my patience." He didn't want to have to kill him. He'd had no sire to teach him their ways and had fed off the children, not by choice, but because it was the only thing presented to him aside from the occasional rat.

Thea stayed where she was, afraid to get closer to any of them. She reached into her coat pockets and brought out the two bags of blood she had taken from Edric's house. "Liam?"

Liam turned to her, crimson eyes and fangs protruding. Thea flinched but handed him the bags. He tossed one to Edric who drank it dry. When Liam threw the second one, Edric got off of Patrick and gave him the bag.

Patrick took it gratefully and devoured it. He looked up at Edric.

The older vampire nodded the answer to the silent question. "Yes, there's more. But you won't be killing anyone tonight."

Thea could not bring herself to watch either of them drink. She fought back tears and wished she was home. She was having a hard time catching her breath and her face felt flush. "We need to go," she said.

"Through there." Edric nodded to the window Liam had created.

Liam jumped up through the opening like a cat. Edric motioned to Patrick to go ahead. Once he had gone, Edric walked over to Thea. "I'll help you up," he said softly.

She said nothing, but turned and allowed him to lift her up. She grabbed Liam's hand and he pulled her the rest of the way. Edric came through in one swift motion. He put his hand on Liam's shoulder. "Thank you, but I need to ask more of you." He looked at the house.

"I'll take care of it Edric."

Edric nodded at his childe. "Give Patrick a place to stay; help him. If he refuses to comply..."

"I'll take care of that too," Liam finished.

Thea pretended not to know what they were talking about and was thankful when Edric put his arm around her and walked back to her car. They were silent while he drove them back to his home in the village.

Chapter 7

Edric turned the car off and looked at her. He gently touched her cheek. She closed her eyes and leaned into his touch. "Thank you," he said to her. He didn't need for her to respond any more than she had when he had touched her face. Her gesture meant the world to him. After what she had been through tonight, she still wanted him near her; she was stronger than he had thought. He got out and walked around to her side, opening her door.

Thea was exhausted, physically and mentally. She wanted nothing more than to lie next to Edric with his arms around her, making her feel safe. She had been trying to make sense out of the night. She had gone to the Arthur home ready to save that wretched old man from a certain hellish life, imprisoned by his vampire son. When she got there she learned he was in fact the warden, not the prisoner, and they ended up saving the vampire instead. She didn't want to think about how Liam and Patrick cleaned up the loose ends, knowing that she would read about it in the paper.

She leaned against Edric as he walked her into the bedroom. She hadn't the strength to even speak. She vaguely wondered if she was in shock.

Edric sat Thea down on the bed. He took off her shoes and socks, before guiding her to lie down and slipping her out of her jeans. He draped the blankets over her. When he turned to leave she grabbed his hand and looked up at him. "I'll be right back, Luv," he promised.

Thea heard the refrigerator door open and close, and then the microwave going. Edric came back a few minutes later, undressed in the dark and slid under the covers next to her. She lay her head into his shoulder and finally felt herself calming down when he wrapped his arms securely around her.

The tension in the room was thick, but Edric waited until he could sense Thea's body had quieted before speaking. He kissed her on top of her head. "You disobeyed me."

"I'm not your childe, I make my own decisions."

"I know," he said, reconsidering his attempt to break the mood. "I'm glad you did. When did you figure it out?"

Thea sat up and turned on the dim lamp on the bedside table. "I thought about how often a... you need to eat, and I thought that maybe David was getting people from other neighborhoods, and then I thought what if there's like this army that you were walking into. So I went down to that bar Friday night– "

"You did what?" Edric shouted as he sat up. "I told you never–"

"I stayed in my car, I knew Liam would come out. Anyway, he said you could take care of yourself but I just knew something was wrong when you didn't come back right away." She paused. "So Saturday I went to the park, and when I saw Mr. Arthur come to sit on that bench I knew for sure something had gone wrong. I went over to him and approached him about doing an interview, and made the appointment for the evening. I brought the bags from your refrigerator because you said it heals you."

"That was very smart of you, Thea."

"And if I hadn't thought to bring them? Would you have..." she let her voice trail off, not sure she wanted to hear the answer. She looked down at her hands.

Edric lifted her chin. "No," he answered, "didn't I tell you I would never hurt you?"

Thea nodded, she felt the sting of tears.

"And have I ever lied to you?"

She shook her head as a tear trailed down her cheek.

"Come here." Edric brought her into his embrace.

Thea let the tears flow then, unable to hold them back. "I went there thinking I could save that old man and he was behind everything. How could I have been so foolish?"

"You see the good in people, Thea. That's not a terrible way to be. Besides, you're safe now." He kissed her forehead and then moved her face to his. "I will *always* keep you safe."

"I know that, Edric, you've proven it over and over, but what you are still frightens me."

"Say it."

She looked up at him puzzled. "Say what?"

"I've never heard you say what I am out loud. Say that I'm a vampire."

Thea shook her head and closed her eyes.

"Not saying it won't make it less true. Say it," he ordered.

Thea didn't open her eyes and when she spoke, she did so in a whisper, "you're a ... vampire."

"Look at me and say it." He felt his demon stir at his dominance over her.

Thea looked in his eyes, relieved they were still blue. "You're a vampire," she breathed.

"Louder," he commanded, his excitement growing. He grabbed her by the back of her head, bringing her lips right up to his.

Thea felt the familiar pleasure of her stomach flipping and her breath came in short gasps when he grabbed her. "You're a vampire," she obeyed.

Edric tightened his grip on her hair and captured her lips in a demanding kiss. He heard her whimper under him and he lightened his grip on her. He brought her back down to the bed and moved on top of her. He wanted to ravage her, to dominate her some more, but he knew she was not ready. He wanted her to stay with him, and after the events of tonight, she needed him to be softer, gentler, to restore her confidence. He eased the tension between them. He could feel the tears on her face, taste the salt on her skin. He secured his demon deep inside his core and made love to her sweetly, allowing her to feel secure with him.

Thea's tears were of relief as the shackles of denial melted away. Feeling a weight lifted from her, she gave in to Edric's advances, enjoying the feel of him, the taste. There was no other place she would rather be than in his arms.

She lay there afterward, head resting in the crook of his shoulder and thought back to Friday night. "Liam says you try to hold onto your humanity, like you're denying what you really are," she broke their silence.

"Liam is young yet, he will learn that it is our power to hold onto our humanity that gives us the strength to become masters of our demons."

"There's so much to know about you," Thea said without looking up at him.

"We have a lifetime, Pet."

Thea let him end the conversation. She didn't want to talk about it anymore. There was time to find out about Edric and this new world she was being brought into by him. She closed her eyes and prayed she would not dream.

Epilogue

"So what's the name of that girl?" Peter turned and looked back at Jonathan who seemed to be having a difficult time of navigating the trail with any amount of grace or speed.

Jonathan caught up to his new friend and caught his breath before answering, "Forsythea Daniels. She was the love of my life."

Peter turned and continued up the trail. "That's too bad, man. C'mon, it's not much further."

Jonathan panted his way through the deep forest that surrounded the Lake George area. He had met Peter last weekend at an engagement party of a mutual friend. Neither one of them had been having all that much of a good time, and they had hit it off over a few beers. Peter had invited Jonathan to a weekend trip of hiking and camping, a proposition that had sounded, at the time, like just the thing Jonathan needed to get his mind off of his fiance up and leaving him. He hadn't realized just how physically taxing the trip would be.

"We'll set up camp here," Peter was saying when Jonathan caught up to him. He looked toward the setting sun with a small smile. "It'll be dark soon," he said.

Jonathan let his pack fall from his aching shoulders and took a deep breath, thankful they had finally stopped. "That's okay, it's a full moon tonight so we'll have plenty of light." He started unloading some supplies. He looked up at Peter who was still watching the sun set. "Hey Peter, aren't you going to unpack your things for the night?"

Peter ignored the question. "Do you want her back, Jonathan?"

"Who? Thea? Of course I do; I love her."

"Then you need to hunt her down and take her."

Jonathan thought then that Peter seemed... bigger... or something. "I don't think she would..."

Peter was smiling wildly when he looked at his unknowing companion. "You are about to be given a gift, Jonathan, a gift of endless power and strength. Anything you want, you will be able to take!" Peter fell to his knees then and grabbed his head as he called out in pain.

Jonathan knelt at his side and placed a hand on his shoulder. "Peter, are you all right?"

His voice turned gruff, "Think of her, Jonathan, while you run."

Jonathan fell back when Peter looked up at him. His eyes had gone from a smoky brown to a cat-like gold and Peter's face had changed, distorted impossibly like in some freakish horror film. Large canines filled his mouth which had started to protrude from his face. "Run, Jonathan," he warned.

Jonathan scrambled to his feet and ran blindly through the trees. He had no idea where the trail had disappeared to and darkness had fallen very quickly in the September sky. He stopped to catch his breath behind a large stone and searched the twilight for a sign of life.

This couldn't be happening. He fought the irrational thoughts coming into his mind. There was no way that he just watched a man turning into some kind of creature, it just couldn't be. Jonathan held his breath. The forest seemed unnaturally quiet.

A loud howl breached the silence and caused Jonathan's very blood to turn cold. He got up to run, vowing this time not to stop because whatever his logical mind told him, he *knew* what Peter had turned into. He managed about ten yards when an enormous creature leaped into his path. Jonathan's heart pounded ferociously and his legs became incredibly weak. The creature stood easily 6 feet tall while still on four limbs. It snarled loudly as it circled its prey.

"Peter...," Jonathan tried.

The werewolf stood on its powerful hind legs then and howled in triumph.

Jonathan did indeed think of Forsythea as he screamed.

Find out what becomes of Jonathan

in Book 2 of

The Community Series:

Lunar Attacks

www.ingramcontent.com/pod-product-compliance
Lightning Source LLC
Chambersburg PA
CBHW051842170626
46807CB00003B/1307